CANDY CAIN
KILLS AGAIN

THE SECOND SLAYING

BRIAN McAULEY

CANDY CAIN KILLS AGAIN

THE SECOND SLAYING

KILLER VHS SERIES
BOOK 5

SHORTWAVE
PUBLISHING

Copyright © 2024 by Brian McAuley

Cover design by Marc Vuletich and Alan Lastufka.
Interior design by Alan Lastufka.

First Edition published November 2024.

10 9 8 7 6 5 4 3 2 1

ISBN 978-1-959565-44-4 (Paperback)
ISBN 978-1-959565-45-1 (eBook)

For the naughty ones.
Again.

PREVIOUSLY ON...

'Twas the night before Christmas, when all through the house
Candy Cain was stirring, the Werners were roused.
But first she took hammer to handyman Rick,
Then realtor Lynette was dropped like a brick.

The friends of sweet Austin appeared to surprise
Before they all met a most grisly demise.
Poor Ethan did choke on a mountain of snow,
And Valerie split between legs and torso.

Pa Greg tried his best to protect his dear fam,
Till the sheriff shot twice, a wolf playing lamb.
Ma Dana was offed with a knife through the head,
Then secrets unfurled, so follow this thread. . .

'Twas not killer Candace returned from the dead,
But good sister Abby, who survived and then fled
To the cellar to hide for ten years of silence,
Then emerged on this day to wreak festive violence.

Fiona escaped with Mateo and Austin,
Drove back to the diner for cocoa, exhausted.
But the story's not over, it's now Christmas Day,
And Candy Cain waits for more presents to play!

CHAPTER ONE

Dear God, it happened again.

The thought keeps spinning in Frank's head as he and the boys sort through the wreckage at the old Thornton house. In his thirty years of service as a firefighter, he's been called to duty at plenty of horrific scenes. From fatal car wrecks to meth lab explosions and every flaming mess in between. But there's only one case that still haunts him to this day. One memory that wakes him in a cold sweat, whole body shaking until Rita coos him back to sleep like a two-hundred-pound baby.

It happened right here, ten years ago, on Christmas Day.

Frank had just made chief a week before the call came through, so he was all the more determined to show his crew what a good leader he could be. His team hustled to the scene and put out that house fire in record time; but before they could assess the damage, that creepy cop stepped out from the shadows.

"I'll take it from here, boys." Dying embers glinted off the sheriff's badge reading *Brock*.

Frank puffed up his chest at the dismissal. "We need to enter first, make sure it's safe to—"

"I appreciate your service." The sheriff's big paw clamped down on Frank's shoulder. "But you are not under the employ of this community. Now, please take your men out of Nodland, and have yourself a merry little Christmas."

Frank wanted to punch the son of a bitch right in his merry mustache, but the thought of his men watching from the sidelines gave him pause. Good chiefs don't punch sheriffs.

"Okay, boys." Frank mustered as much authority as he could, acting like it was his decision. "Let's pack it up."

He knew there was something off about that lawman, about the whole town of Nodland. They did things their own way, and every other town in the county knew that well.

Just leave Nodland be.

But that little hamlet was too small for its own fire department, so Frank had no regrets about crossing community lines to lend a thankless hand.

No, the regrets would come a week later.

Rita had fixed him a big breakfast before his day shift while he sat at the kitchen table with his morning paper. When he saw the *Candy Cain Killings* headline, he puked right there into his scrambled eggs and bacon. According to the article, it wasn't just a fire that killed the Thornton family.

It was murder.

Frank stewed with that awful knowledge until

another week passed, and that same paper issued a retraction, blaming a drug-addled medical examiner for the misinformation. Nothing more than a tree fire. Nothing to see here.

Just leave Nodland be.

Even Rita was pushing him to let sleeping dogs lie, saying it wasn't Frank's concern. But the way the whole story unfolded and then folded back up again left an ick in his gut that just wouldn't unstick. He couldn't help feeling guilty, like if he'd stayed on the scene, insisted on finishing his investigation, then maybe they'd all know what the hell really happened at the Thornton house back in '95.

But he didn't, and now he's standing here ten years later, looking at the crumbled remnants of the house he couldn't save. The mystery he couldn't solve.

The only thing Frank knows for sure this time is that the sheriff won't be coming to stand in his way. Because that's definitely the local lawman's headless corpse beneath the burned-out vehicle in front of him. The other bodies scattered in the snow tell a grim story that Frank can't quite piece together, but he will. This time, he'll get to the truth himself.

Frank's not a religious man by any stretch of the imagination, not like Rita, who prays nightly, but he does believe in some kind of fate. Something had drawn him back to the scene of a crime he'd failed to solve ten years ago.

Now he's got a chance to make it right.

He circles around the rubble to find Dave shoveling stones from the collapsed cellar. The buff gym rat's treating it like a workout, doing heave-ho reps with perfect form.

"Find anything?" Frank asks.

Dave points his shovel into the debris. "Looks like two more bodies down here, stuffed into a floor hatch."

The collapsed stones must've protected their flesh from the flames, but some of the damage Frank's seeing is clearly the work of a human hand. Falling stones don't slice your guts open and wrap your insides around your outside.

"Let's leave them for EMS." Frank wants to make sure he does everything by the book here, no contaminations or loose ends.

Not too far from Dave is Little Jimmy, still spraying the hose from the truck, making sure the flames are out for good. The poor kid can hardly bear the strength of the kickback with his stringy arms, but he's come a long way under Frank's guidance.

"Jimmy, how we looking?"

The rookie cranks the hose off and flips his protective mask up to reveal that boyish face, dripping with sweat. "All clear... I think."

Jimmy's eyes fall to the snowy ground, and Frank follows his gaze to the torso of that poor dead girl. Looks like an animal ripped her in half at the waist, but the shard of glass sticking from her guts tells Frank she likely had a bad date with a broken window.

"Frank. . ." Jimmy's voice cracks as he asks, "What the hell happened here?"

The kid's too new to know the legend, but Frank

can't stop the thought that's already crawling around his brain.

Candy Cain came home.

He snuffs it out the moment he thinks it. Never let an ember grow into a flame, like the one that just started flickering in the rubble at Jimmy's feet.

"Not your job to figure that out, son," Frank says. It's *his* job, his calling. "Your job is to make sure we keep that fire out."

He points at the blossoming flame. Jimmy scrambles to lower his mask, flipping the hose back on and dousing the glowing embers with fresh water.

The bodies are gruesome, yes, but Frank's gut tells him that the answer lies where a body doesn't. He walks back over to that curious human-shaped dent in the snow. Bending down to inspect the blackened snow angel, Frank's sure somebody burned here, no doubt about that. But where'd they fly off to?

Amidst the black ash on white snow, Frank's eyes catch on a little spot of red, lodged in the angel's wing. He plucks the scrap of charred cloth, rubbing his thumb to clear the soot as the pattern beneath brightens.

Red and white stripes.

Like a candy cane.

Before his next fearful thought can take hold, there's a heavy tap-tap-tap on his right shoulder. Frank swallows hard, turning his head to see the tip of the iron fire poker resting there, hook side up.

"We three kings of orient are!"

The voice behind him is hoarse and off-key, but oozing with so much joy.

"Bearing gifts, we traverse afar!"

Frank's been caught on his knees, totally disarmed. The most he can do is reach up to lower his face mask like a gladiator preparing for battle before he shifts around on bent knee to face his fate.

"Field and fountain!"

The first thing he sees are those red and white striped pajamas, shredded and scorched. Her skin is flash-charred like a fancy steak with raw pink pulsing through the black cracks. That degree of burn would leave any normal human being screaming in endless agony.

"Moor and mountain!"

But Candy Cain is smiling as she sings.

"Following yonder star!"

CHAPTER TWO

The First King is kneeling in front of me while I sing, gripping the fire poker.

"Born a King on Bethlehem's plain!"

It hurts to smile, skin splitting at the edges of my mouth, but I grin through the pain to welcome him to my own little Bethlehem.

The King doesn't smile back. His face twists in disgust behind the clear mask, and I shrink back, ashamed. Why would a king come all this way, bearing gifts on Christmas Day, only to make me feel so ugly?

My hand tightens around the golden handle of the fire poker as I remember what Mother always said.

It's better to give than to receive.

"Gold I bring to crown Him again!"

I bend my arm back, preparing my offering as the First King's last word fogs the glass.

"Rita."

I don't know her.

The iron spike thrusts forward. It cracks through the mask and *squelches* into the king's nose, deeper and deeper until it breaks free on the other side and only the golden handle is left sticking out from his face.

"King forever, ceasing never!"

The First King stumbles to his feet, grasping at his new nose like a golden carrot on an off-kilter snowman. But the long poker is too heavy, weighing down the back of his head until the king falls backwards in the snow. When the tip hits the ground, the whole poker gets pushed back up out of his face with a fresh *slurrip!*

"Over us all to reign!"

"Frank!" screams the Second King. No helmet or mask, all muscles and rage.

"Frankincense to offer have I!"

But I don't see any frankincense in this king's hands. Only a shovel.

"Incense owns a Deity high!"

The Second King swings his bad present, but I duck and stick out my leg to trip him. A trick the kids in Bible school often used on my sister. It worked then and it works now as the Second King falls face first in the white powder. He rolls onto his back, coughing up snow, and I've already got a hold of his shovel.

"Prayer and praising!"

This angry snowman needs a happy new smile. I raise the shovel high, sharp edge pointed down. He opens his mouth wide to scream, giving me an easier target as the curved blade slams down between his top and bottom teeth.

"All men raising!"

I guess I dug too deep for the Second King's smile

because when I pry the shovel back, the top half of his head breaks off and rolls away like a bloody kickball.

"Worship him, God most high!"

"Jesus fucking Christ!" cries another voice.

I look around, but see no savior. Only the foul-mouthed Third King, tossing a big hose to the ground. The scrawny boy pulls his mask off, tears streaming down his face.

This final king looks kinder, softer. Maybe I'll finally get a real gift from him.

"You killed them!" he screams. "You killed them!"

Doesn't he know that death is only the beginning?

He charges across the snow, head low and arms wide, aiming to tackle me.

Not very king-like at all.

I twirl on my feet, dropping low to swing the shovel against the skinny king's kneecap. It *snaps* like peanut brittle, and he falls on all fours to moan and wail.

If none of these kings are here to bring me gifts, then I'll just have to take one for myself.

"Myrrh is mine, its bitter perfume!"

Maybe there's myrrh in that big hose. I pick it up and hold the nozzle an inch away from the Third King's face. When I pull the lever back, a blast of high-pressured water rips the skin from his skull in one slick sheet, like wrapping paper getting torn off a present.

The Third King screams, pawing at his unwrapped face, all red and wet.

"Breathes a life of gathering gloom!"

No myrrh in there, but I'm not giving up yet.

There's a whole cabinet full of shiny toys on the fire

truck. I skip over to make my pick, but it's so hard to choose just one. The handheld fire extinguisher looks like the most fun, so I pluck it from the hook and hurry back to the Third King.

He's sitting back on his shins with red running down the front of his uniform. I aim the black hose at his bloody face and squeeze the handle, but it doesn't budge.

The Third King's lidless eyes stare as he reaches up a shaky finger and points at the silver ring hanging from the handle.

Silly me. Safety first.

Pulling the ring frees the pin, and I squeeze the handle with all my might. A blast of white bursts out like chemical confetti, coating the red meat where the king's face once was.

"Sorrowing, sighing!"

More like coughing, gagging.

"Bleeding, dying!"

Until the Third King finally stops making all those unhappy sounds.

"Sealed in the stone cold tomb!"

Hunched in a seated position with his upper body all caked in white, this is the best snowman I've made yet. But when I look around the quiet lawn, there's no one left to admire it with me. Nothing moves except the smoke rising from the ashes that was once my home.

Good. I hated that place.

Home meant pain. Parents who judged me and stifled my voice. A cellar cage that trapped me for ten long years, cold and alone with nothing to keep me company but the Bible I read over and over and over again.

Until that family arrived and awakened me from my tomb.

"Glorious now behold Him arise!"

A fire was lit in my frozen heart, a fire that still burns bright.

"King and God and Sacrifice!"

All the memories I'd tucked away in the trap door of my mind are stirring to the surface now.

Memories that won't stay hidden any longer.

Memories with feelings attached.

"Alleluia, alleluia!"

Anger, anger, anger, anger!

"Heaven to earth replies!"

The sun is rising in the sky, and I can't look away.

"O star of wonder, star of night!"

It burns hot in my vision, meeting the flames within.

"Star with royal beauty bright!"

I want to share this fire with the world, with the one who molded me like Adam from the clay.

The dawn of a new day means it's Christmas morning.

Christmas morning means it's time for church.

I climb behind the wheel of the big red fire truck, engine still rumbling with life. It can't be all that different from riding a tricycle, can it? My long legs just barely reach the pedals as I press my bare right foot on the widest one.

The truck doesn't move.

Only one other option. When my foot presses the

right pedal, the truck leaps to life and I pull the big wheel, aiming the rig down the long driveway.

When I see the *Thornton* mailbox, I tug the wheel hard to the left, knocking the wooden post from its roots as the truck skids out onto the empty road.

"Westward leading, still proceeding!"

I follow the big star toward Nodland, bringing my inner inferno.

"Guide us to thy perfect light!"

Candy Cain is coming to town.

CHAPTER THREE

"**C**andy Cain is dead!"

Pastor Wendell is still puzzling over that outsider boy's words as he stands alone in the church rectory. Reaching for the decanter of wine from the small altar, he swigs straight from the glass with a trembling hand. He wishes he'd kept his mouth shut at the diner last night when he heard that family was staying at the Thornton house, but he couldn't keep quiet for the guilt.

No, not guilt. Wendell isn't guilty, hasn't done anything wrong. He was merely being a good Samaritan to those outsiders, giving them fair warning.

Not that he really believes the Thornton place is haunted. When a person dies, it's Heaven or Hell for their spirit. There is no in between. It's just that every Christmas, the fear comes creeping up that somehow a reckoning will come.

But what's there to reckon with? Pastor Wendell is a good man, and he washes that truth down with another sip of wine.

Ten years ago, he was sure that everything he built

here in Nodland would come crashing down, but God willed otherwise. That's how Wendell knows he's on the path of righteousness.

It was a mess, Lord knows, but that's what Sheriff Brock was anointed for. Nodland's humble servant helped to tidy things up back then so that Wendell's church could live on. A sacred mission such as his requires dedicated apostles.

Of course, he didn't always know his mission with such clarity. There was a time when Wendell was just as lost as the rest of the heathens.

Born under the name Robert Mulligan into a house full of drunkards in South Boston, he sought solace in the Catholic Church. Starting as an altar boy, he worked his way up to become the youngest priest in the diocese. He reveled in the ceremonies of Catholicism, all the flesh and the blood, but it didn't take long before congregants complained that his sermons focused too much on the Old Testament.

After getting bounced around New England from one church to the next, he was finally excommunicated for his "extreme interpretations" of the Bible. Hypocrites, those Catholic priests. He saw what so many of them did behind closed doors, and it was a whole lot worse than preaching proper liturgy.

Luckily, he found a Baptist church in South Carolina that was much more welcoming of his fire and brimstone speeches. But folks in those churches seemed far too focused on joy and celebration. Where was the fear, the wrath of the Lord? Traveling onward, he found the fervor he was seeking in the Pentecostal tents of the Mississippi swamplands.

He developed quite a following in one remote parish, stoking a primordial connection with savagery, until a local child died of a snakebite in the middle of a cleansing ceremony. The people blamed *him*, their humble pastor. As if the child's death wasn't a clear case of God's judgment upon an unfit follower. The local law got involved, and he became a wanted man. That's when he took up the mantle of his new name, Wendell Wake, and set out on the road again, bound for Texas.

By then, the American Evangelical movement was seeing a great boom; and as far as Wendell could tell, the rules were a whole lot looser in that sect. You could customize your church, your community, however you saw fit.

Unfortunately, the Evangelical preachers were much more devoted to the material world than they were to divinity. Weak little men all tangled up in politics and wealth, seeking social power to feed their egos and bank accounts. None of them were devout enough to truly understand and preach scripture the way Wendell did, to guide humanity away from those earthly traps. None of them possessed the righteous faith necessary to inherit the kingdom of Heaven.

But Pastor Wendell would not give up. He spent his whole life as a spiritual pilgrim, a God-fearing Goldilocks in search of the perfect fit, until his true mission was finally revealed to him.

He was wandering his way through the mountains of California, aiming for the coast when a sudden snowstorm hit. Lost and alone, he sought refuge in an old abandoned church with broken pews and empty aisles. While knelt in solemn prayer, feeling utterly forsaken, a strange light shone through the dingy stained-glass window. God spoke to him, told him that this was his home now. Told him who he really was.

The next morning, after the storm passed, what Wendell found outside those church doors was a tiny mountain hamlet, desperate for direction. With only one road in or out, Nodland couldn't be found unless you were really looking for it. The resorts of Big Bear were just far enough to draw all the tourists that way and keep outsiders at bay.

It was here that Wendell would finally build his own church, raise his own flock.

Commence the great cleansing.

"Pastor Wendell?" Timothy appears in the doorway, blonde hair perfectly parted. "Do you need help?"

The eighteen-year-old boy reminds Wendell so much of his younger self, which is why he makes such a good youth pastor.

"No, Timothy." Wendell caps the wine decanter. "I was just making sure we had enough wine for the service." His service was special, as he'd taken the best parts of each religion he encountered and created something new, something pure in the Church of Nodland.

"I refilled the decanter last night." Timothy moves to the armoire and pulls out a crisp red sash. "And ironed your Christmas stole." He drapes the cloth around Wendell's shoulders.

"Bless you, child. Let us not keep them waiting."

They exit the rectory into the Sunday school classroom, then down the steps into the kitchen. The old church has its own odd geography, a labyrinth of stone like some medieval castle, but Wendell much prefers the ancient weight of this place to those glittery Walmart super-churches.

In the narrow kitchen, Nash is already hard at work preparing the community meal. The cook was a broken man when Wendell found him, traumatized by his service overseas. But once Wendell put that soldier's hands to work, they were filled with the Lord's purpose.

"Looks like we'll be having quite the feast today, Nash."

The cook beams with pride. "This day shall be for you a memorial day, and you shall keep it as a feast to the Lord."

Wendell nods at the verse and surveys the food. "I don't see Marjorie's famous stew."

"She hasn't arrived yet."

"So unlike her," Wendell responds. "Here's hoping we don't miss out."

"Yes." Nash gives a knowing grin, having bonded with the pastor over their secret distaste for Marjorie's stew. "Here's hoping."

Wendell pats the cook on his shoulder and moves toward the far door.

"Away in a manger, no crib for a bed!"

On the other side, his congregation sings to Isaac's beautiful organ music.

Candy Cain is dead!

That outsider boy's nonsense words pop back into

his mind, but Pastor Wendell quickly shakes them out. This is not her day. It's His day.

"The little Lord Jesus lay down his sweet head!"

And a glorious day it shall be.

He opens the door and steps out onto the altar.

"The stars in the sky look down where he—"

The moment he approaches his lectern, the music cuts out mid-chord and the room falls silent. One of the many rules of his handcrafted service. When the pastor is ready to speak, there shall be no sound. Only reverent silence, listening to the Lord's chosen vessel.

The pews aren't full, but they never are. It's a small community, humble, but they're working on growing through the youth program. Once the children are properly trained, they will head off on their own missions to cleanse the heathen world. Nodland may be a speck on the map now, but His kingdom will come for all.

Pastor Wendell smiles at his flock.

"Merry Christmas, fine people of Nodland. Today we celebrate the birth of our Lord and savior, Jesus Christ. Born of the Virgin Mary with no earthly father, and thus, no sin in his heart. God gave us His only son to undo the damage caused by the fall of Adam, the corruption of innocence. Indeed, Jesus Christ is a prophecy fulfilled, the destiny of his very existence rooted in his inevitable death."

"That is why, on this holy day, we celebrate not only his birth. . . but his death, long and full of pain. For if we know not his pain, we know not his love. We live because he died for us, but the story does not end there. Only one being on this earth has ever been prophesied to return, to rise from the grave and save us all again."

"Only you, my faithful flock, bear the wisdom that this fateful return has already transpired. You know that your savior is here, that Christ incarnate will lead you to righteous absolution."

This truth is reflected back to him through their adoring eyes.

"He is reborn of new flesh. . ."

Pastor Wendell opens his arms wide. A living legend.

"The Second Coming."

CHAPTER FOUR

Sitting in the diner booth after the longest night of his life, Mateo isn't really sure what Austin means when he says, "Why don't we have one more cup of cocoa, then go to church and raise some hell?"

But Fiona seems all for it as she smiles with an, "Amen."

"What kind of hell are we talking about here?" Mateo finally asks, nervously gripping his mug.

Fiona stares out the window, across the street at the grey stone church with the tall bell tower. "We're gonna burn that place to the ground."

Mateo nearly chokes on his cocoa. "What?!"

"Fiona, no!" Austin gratefully clarifies. "I was just talking about confronting the congregation."

"Right, totally." Fiona blushes and sips from her mug. "I meant, like. . . metaphorically burn it down."

"Either way, I really don't see the point," Mateo says.

"Speaking of seeing the point. . ." Fiona gestures to the broken candy cane ornament still protruding from Mateo's eye. "You feeling okay?"

The adrenaline pumping through Mateo's blood must have been keeping the pain at bay, but the reminder of his new facial accessory seems to flush that chemical relief away now. His eye socket throbs around the jagged porcelain as Austin takes him by the hand.

"Come on. Let's get you fixed up." Austin guides Mateo to the counter, shouting through the order window at Grace in the kitchen. "Hey, Grace? You have a first aid kit back there?"

"Sure thing, sweetie," the waitress calls from out of sight, then comes through the swinging door holding a metal box that looks like it's been rusting under a sink since the '70s.

"Bathroom?" Austin asks, and Grace points around the corner. Mateo can't help noticing a shift in Austin, the way he's taking charge with new confidence as they squeeze into the tiny bathroom.

"Sit." Austin motions to the toilet seat.

Mateo lowers himself onto it, looks up into the flickering fluorescent bulb above. "Just try not to get any rust dust in my eye, please."

"This is probably gonna hurt. Like, a lot." Austin places an uncapped bottle of antiseptic spray in Mateo's hand. "You ready?"

Mateo shrugs. "Can't be festive forever." Because what else can he do in this moment but crack a dumb joke?

Austin's hand wraps around the candy cane as Mateo commands: "Yank that fucker ou—" Yank. "—owww, dude!"

Pain pulses through his skull, and Mateo is no longer seeing fluorescents. Only stars.

"Sorry!" Austin says. "I thought it'd be easier without a whole countdown."

Mateo blindly sprays the antiseptic into the wound. Annoyingly, it's not a continuous spray nozzle, but a puny pump-pump-pump situation, so he keeps pump-pump-pumping until the whole area goes numb. The stuff actually works pretty well, so he's hopeful it's not expired, but he's not about to check the date on the bottle either.

His one good eye finally comes back into focus, staring at the bloody point of the candy cane ornament still clutched in Austin's hand. Mateo's afraid to ask, but he has to ask: "Is my eye still. . . in there?"

Austin squints into Mateo's face. "It's in there, yeah. It just kind of looks like a squashed grape."

"Okay, well that's more detail than I was really looking for."

"Sorry! But it's not bleeding." Austin gently wipes the wound with gauze. "So, I think that's good?" He presses a fresh pad over the eyehole and starts wrapping the bandage around Mateo's head. It feels good to be taken care of. Once he's all wrapped up, Mateo reaches for the porcelain ornament.

"Give me that thing."

Austin hands it over, and Mateo feels the delicate weight of it. How could something so fragile cause so much damage? Salty tears are welling in their ducts, causing the squashed-grape socket to sting again.

Mateo smashes the ornament against the ground. "Fuck Candy Cain."

Austin's reply is soft, but pointed. "It's not her fault."

"It's not her *fault?*" Mateo can't believe what he's hearing.

"I just mean. . . she was a victim before she was a killer."

"Why are you defending her?"

"I'm not defending her, but. . ." Austin clearly isn't sure either as he searches for the words. "You didn't meet that pastor like Fiona and I did. The guy reeks of guilt, and the look in his eye this morning when I said Candy Cain was dead. . . There's more to the story, I just know it."

Mateo means his next two words with every ounce of his being: "So what?"

"So, we're just gonna pop into that church, get some answers, and then get you straight to the hospital. Ten minutes, tops."

"I lost my eye, Austin."

"I lost my parents."

Mateo hates him for playing that trump card, but Austin's the one tearing up now. There's got to be a better reason for why he's being so damn stubborn.

"Hey." Mateo takes his hand. "What's this really about?"

Austin's gaze lowers to the tile floor, to the scattered shards of red and white porcelain. "My dad, he never spoke up. . . to anyone. It drove my mom crazy, and they always fought about it. I love him and I miss him. . . but I don't want to be like him." He looks up at Mateo. "I don't want *us* to be like *them*. And I don't want to regret it forever if I don't speak up and take a stand today."

Maybe it's the antiseptic seeping through his eyehole straight into his brain, but Mateo finally gets it, possibly even appreciates it as he relents with a sigh. "Fine. Ten minutes, then we're leaving Nodland in the dust."

Austin squeezes his hand. "Thank you."

"You're welcome." Mateo stands. "Cue *Give 'Em Hell, Kid*."

Austin laughs, and Mateo just can't wait to be back in LA, blasting emo music as they drive around together. But will everything change now that they've shared their true feelings?

He ignores the thought as they exit the gross-ass bathroom to find Fiona comforting a weepy Grace at the counter.

"What's going on?" Austin asks.

"She saw Rick's truck," Fiona explains. "I had to tell her."

Grace uses her apron to dab at the tears in her eyes. "He was just a friend, but I guess I thought that maybe, someday. . ." She clears her throat, shakes her head. "Stupid. Anyway, it sounds like you've all had a real rough night."

"We sure have," Austin says. "And we'd love to get home. You think Rick would mind if we kept his truck?"

Grace looks out the window at the vehicle. "He got it from his dad, who got it from *his* dad. Only right it gets passed down again. Where you headed?"

"Los Angeles," Austin responds.

Grace puts a hand over her heart. "That's where Rick

and I always. . ." She swallows hard. "Do you think I could hitch a ride?"

Mateo's thinking about how cramped that cab is gonna be when Fiona says, "The more the merrier."

Grace smiles, then "Oh!" She goes to the kitchen window, pulling a to-go container. "Don't forget your blueberry pancakes, honey."

Fiona takes the container from her. "You're an angel, Grace."

Mateo and Austin just watch as Fiona pops the container open and douses the pancakes in syrup. Once she's poured a solid gallon in, she turns to them with a shrug.

"What? I'm a growing girl." She closes the lid, puts the Styrofoam container in the plastic bag and turns to Grace. "Back in a bit. Just have to say a few prayers before we roll."

When they step outside, the bright sun has already started turning the snow into icy slicks across the road. Mateo and Austin help Fiona with her cane as they cross the street and approach the bottom of the long church staircase.

Mateo reads the sign: "Nodland Church of Righteous Absolution. What denomination even *is* this place?"

He looks up at the stone structure and secretly makes the sign of the cross. Mateo was raised Catholic, and if his mother knew what he was about to do (whatever it was he was about to do), she would be mortified.

They make their way up the steps, passing a cheesy plastic nativity scene as they push the heavy wooden doors open with a conspicuously loud *creeeaaak*.

". . .the Second Coming," says the pastor in the pulpit, just before every head swivels in the pews to face the trio in the doorway.

The silence is thick before Austin cuts it with a jovial "Merry Christmas," leading Mateo and Fiona down the aisle.

No response. Only watchful eyes.

Mateo can't bear to look at any of them, instead directing his attention to the stained-glass windows in the stone walls. They're not like the ones at his family's church in LA. Same style, sure, but the church windows back home are filled with hopeful, heavenly imagery. What Mateo's looking at now are scenes of Biblical carnage, all blood and fire and brimstone.

What the hell is this place?

"May I help you?" the pastor asks as Austin approaches the pulpit.

"Sorry, Pastor." Austin edges the old man away from the lectern and leans into the microphone. "The power of Christ compels me."

CHAPTER FIVE

Marjorie wishes she'd started the stew sooner. It wasn't her fault the storm blew out her electricity in the middle of the night, killing her alarm clock. Leaping out of bed at five in the morning, an hour behind schedule, she started slicing the beef before her coffee even finished brewing. The vegetable chopping would've taken less time if she had one of those fancy vegetable chopping machines, but Marjorie believed in doing everything by hand.

She's got one eye on the stove clock now and one on the wooden spoon as she does her hopefully final taste test. The thing about stew is you can't make it stew any faster than the time it takes to stew. Luckily, this stew is just right. Thick, but not too thick with the meat cooked through and the paprika popping.

Getting to church on time is going to be a hustle, but she's glad she didn't give up on making her signature dish today. Nash will be cooking up his usual feast, but Pastor Wendell always says Marjorie's stew is his favorite, and she can't disappoint the man.

God, he's brilliant! Handsome too. But that's as far as

she'll let her thoughts go, lest she stray into lust. At sixty-three, she's saved herself this long for Christ, so she must keep her thoughts and actions pure.

Only holy thoughts occupy her mind as she makes the short drive to the little church parking lot, unsurprised to find it's already full. She is officially late now, and Marjorie hates being late. She likes to be in the front row to hear Isaac's glorious organ music up close, letting the sacred songs reverberate in her soul.

She has no choice but to pull into the diner parking lot across the street, where that waitress Grace is smoking a cigarette on the stoop. Marjorie gets out of the car and shakes her head.

"Really, Grace? Right across the street from the Lord's house?"

"Last I checked, cigarettes aren't a sin." Grace exhales smoke. "Besides, I'm getting out of this town for good today."

Marjorie had already warned Pastor Wendell that Grace was going wayward. That outsider handyman was always in the diner, chatting her up, probably filling her head with heathen nonsense.

"She needs to be brought back into line," Marjorie said during a recent confessional.

To which Pastor Wendell responded: "I think all Grace needs is a little grace."

God, what a poet he is! Marjorie thinks on those words now as she extends an olive branch to the smokestack waitress.

"Why don't you come on over to church, honey? Through Him all things are healed."

"If only that were true." Grace stamps out her cigarette. "Merry Christmas, Marjorie. Have a nice life."

Grace heads back into the diner, leaving Marjorie dumbfounded. That poor girl needs Jesus, but it's not Marjorie's job to save her soul today. It's her job to get this stew to the kitchen.

She opens the passenger side door to retrieve the Le Creuset pot resting on the seat. Normally, she only buys American, but nobody makes cookware like the French. Even if they are a country full of wine-swigging fornicators.

Sliding her oven mitts on, she carries the full pot across the street. The road has slicked over with ice, so she has to take it very slow. The pot feels hotter than Hades, even through the mitts, but she just has to make it to the kitchen door at the back of the church. When she finally does, she finds two feet of snow piled up at the door, gleaming in the morning sun.

Dang it, Nash. He should've cleared that path by now.

Marjorie's arms are getting tired from holding the heavy French ceramic. She steels herself before heading back around toward the front of the church. The nativity scene next to the front door beckons her as she gazes up the long staircase. It's not proper, but she has no choice but to bring this food straight into the church. Surely Pastor Wendell will understand.

Marjorie only makes it up the first two steps before she hears the screeching tires.

She stops and turns toward the end of Main Street. A big red fire truck is screaming down the road, swerving to and fro. Nodland doesn't have its own fire department, which means whoever's behind the wheel is an outsider. No wonder they're driving like a maniac. But the lights and sirens aren't blaring, so what's the rush?

Marjorie steps back down to the edge of the sidewalk to shout. "Slow the heck down!"

The truck stops swerving, and Marjorie would be pleased... if it wasn't driving straight toward her now.

She tries to scurry up the steps, but she's just too slow. The fire truck *thumps* over the curb, and that huge metal fender crashes into Marjorie's back with a *snap* of the spine.

Even as she falls beneath the big wheels, her eyes are focused on the pot flying out of her oven-mitted hands as a bitter thought fills her brain.

There goes the stew.

CHAPTER SIX

A festive red pattern splatters across my windshield when the fire truck thumps against the woman's body. I press my foot to the other pedal, bringing the rig to a screeching halt at the bottom of the church steps.

Not bad for my first self-taught driving lesson. I wasn't planning on running anyone over, but something about the way that woman was shouting at me drew me right to her.

I climb out of the truck to find her twisted body twitching on the steps, all bent out of shape like a discarded doll. Leaning down toward her scraped up face, I recognize this old woman. My memory is a dark well, but a bucket is lowering into the depths now to retrieve a name...

Marjorie.

Yes, I remember Marjorie.

She always sat in the front row at Sunday service, and every week she would glare and growl at Candace for fidgeting in the pew behind her. One day, Marjorie finally pulled Mother and Father aside.

"That child is a menace. You need to fix her, get her right in the eyes of the Lord. Make her a good girl, like sweet Abby here."

The woman patted me on the head like a puppy.

Good girl. Good girl. Good girl.

Those two words used to play on repeat in my head. A reminder, a warning. I mustn't ever be bad like my sister.

After church that day, Mother and Father locked Candace in the cellar, in her Bad Girl Box, saying she could come out when she learned to stop fidgeting. I always missed my sister when they took her away like that. I miss her now, but I feel closer to Candace than I ever have as Marjorie sputters on the church steps.

". . .Candace?" the broken woman asks, looking up at me and seeing the sister she so hated.

I shake my head.

". . .Abby?"

I shake my head again.

Good girl is gone now. I've shed my skin like the snake in the garden. Become something else, something more. "Candy Cain."

I look past the woman's bent arm to the pot shattered to bits on the stone steps. Marjorie's famous beef stew is spilled out and steaming in the snow. I always hated that stew. The meat was so tough and chewy, but I'm so very hungry now. After ten years of eating cold tins of deviled ham in the dark cellar, a hot meal is just what my body needs.

I grab the unbroken pot lid by its little black handle.

Like a cymbal, only much heavier. Turning back to Marjorie, I'm ready to make peace with her.

"And in despair I bowed my head. 'There is no peace on Earth,' I said."

I raise the pot lid high.

"For hate is strong and mocks the song."

"Please. . ." Marjorie says. A boring prayer.

"Of peace on Earth, good will to men."

"Be a good gir—"

The lid comes down hard against Marjorie's face, releasing a wet crunch.

"But the bells are ringing!"

A dark red line runs down her forehead, like a crack in the sidewalk filling with blood.

"Peace on Earth!"

Another blow makes the gap grow even wider, jagged white bone now visible.

"Like a choir singing!"

One more cymbal smash caves her face in along the break, and I toss the pot lid aside.

"Peace on Earth!"

Reaching my greedy fingers into Marjorie's split skull, I pry it all the way open like a walnut.

"Does anybody hear them?"

I cup my hand like a ladle to scoop out a handful of scrambled egg brains, raising the fresh meal to my lips.

"Peace on Earth!"

The gooey meat fills my mouth, so tender I barely have to chew. I've forgotten how good a hot meal can feel, spreading warmth down into my stomach, then out to the tips of my fingers and toes. I swallow several more handfuls of pinkish jelly until the woman's head is an empty shell. It wasn't a very big brain.

With the *ding* of a bell, a waitress rushes out of the diner across the street. She takes one look at me, crouched and feeding on Marjorie's corpse, then rushes back inside, flipping the *Closed* sign.

Let her close. I'm full anyway, my body reenergized.

The long church steps are calling me now toward those big wooden doors with the nativity scene beside them. It's Jesus's birthday, and I can't miss the party. I grab a present from the fire truck and start up the staircase.

I've climbed these steps so many times before, but never alone. Always with Candace's hand held tight in mine. Gripping the present in my left hand now, I hold out my right one for her, imagining she's with me. I'll need her strength today.

"The wrong shall fail, the right prevail
With peace on Earth, good will to men!"

CHAPTER SEVEN

I t's cold in the church, but Austin is sweating in the face of a few dozen congregants now staring expectantly at him. He'd been imagining them as a faceless mass, but now that he's standing at the podium, looking out at a mix of men, women, and children, it's harder to process how real they all are. How human.

He hasn't exactly prepared a speech for this big moment, so he just starts with the basics.

"My name is Austin Werner. That's my sister Fiona."

He points to Fiona, who sits in the front pew, cracking open her Styrofoam container. She gives him an encouraging thumbs up before stabbing her plastic fork down and taking a syrupy bite of pancakes.

"And this is Mateo." He motions to Mateo, standing off to the side of the altar. "My boyfriend." They all look so scandalized by the proclamation that he can't help doubling-down with: "My *gay* boyfriend." Just in case they missed the point.

The disapproval in their faces only fuels his purpose.

"My family stayed at the Thornton house last night."

Gasps from the pews as some of them make the sign

of the cross. To Austin, the gesture is nothing more than an admission of guilt.

"Yeah. You know the place. I guess it's your local haunted house now. But before that, it was a home. To members of *your* congregation."

The congregants avert their eyes, well-trained in their collective ignorance.

"You knew what was happening there, didn't you?" Austin needles them now, pointing his finger into the crowd. It's a rhetorical question, but he can't help hoping for a confession. Just one. "You knew that Candace Thornton was being abused by her parents."

Images from that terrible videotape flash behind Austin's eyes. He thought *he* had bad parents, but now he knows they're saints in comparison.

They *were* saints.

He still hasn't processed the reality that Mom and Dad are gone now.

No, not gone. That's too passive.

Taken.

Austin would be sad if he wasn't so damn pissed off. He's ready to spit lava and drown the whole damn church in his rage when Pastor Wendell steps up to the podium and interrupts.

"Okay, young man. You've spoken your piece. And yes, of course we knew there was trouble in that house. We take care of our own here in Nodland, as best we can. But you can't possibly blame a whole community for the actions of two wayward individuals." The old man is sweating last night's whiskey as he tries to defend himself. "God gave them free will, same as all of us."

"And you used your free will to turn a blind eye," Austin says. "You did nothing to stop—"

"I *tried!*" Pastor Wendell shouts, losing his composure as he holds up a trembling finger. It's not whiskey Austin smells on his breath now, but wine. Is this guy ever sober? "I tried everything in my power to stop that evil. But some souls simply cannot be saved."

"Yeah." Austin stares the pastor directly in the eye. "I'm looking at one of them."

The whole church erupts in murmurs at the disrespect, but Wendell just seems annoyed at the disruption as he sighs deeply.

"Why are you here?" he asks. "Interrupting our sacred service on Christmas morning, drudging up the past like this?"

Mateo steps forward. "Because the past came back. Candy Cain killed again."

Fear creeps into the pastor's countenance for a split second before he blinks it away and forces a weak laugh. "I don't know what kind of prank you're playing at. . ." He turns to the congregation, as if to reassure them along with himself. ". . .but Candy Cain is nothing more than make believe."

"Kinda like the Bible?" Fiona chimes in from her front row seat. The pew people behind her do not like that, but she doesn't care, pointing her plastic fork at the pastor. "You're the one who warned us about her last night."

"Ah." Wendell blushes, leaning into the microphone. "I'm afraid I must confess that I let the spirits possess me last night. Not a sin, mind you, to indulge in modest libations on the eve of a holy day. But in such a state, I sometimes become unduly fearful of ghosts."

Austin can see how this slick-talking pastor has managed to get where he is, dodging responsibility with his slippery words.

"We're not talking about a ghost," Mateo says, pointing at his bandaged eye. "We're talking about a flesh and blood killer, because Candy Cain has risen."

The church doors kick in, and a cold wind whistles down the aisle.

Austin shields his eyes from the blinding daylight with a hand in front of his face. He squints through his fingers against the bright white, barely making out the silhouette in the doorway, backlit and glowing like some holy saint.

A saint gripping a cherry red fire axe with a white-striped blade.

Austin shudders as the figure comes into focus.

This can't be happening. It can't be her.

The word "No. . ." slips from his lips and catches in the microphone. It echoes up into the vaulted ceiling, reverberating in the cavernous space.

"No, no, no, no, no. . ."

But this simple prayer won't stop what comes next.

Candy Cain steps across the church threshold, and Hell follows with her.

CHAPTER EIGHT

The moment my bare feet hit the cold church floor, I'm drowning in memories. This place, these people. All the pain these walls contained. The faces in the pews turning to look my way now may be ten years older, but I know them, and they know me.

Except for the young children.

In the Church of Nodland, children don't have a voice. They are meant to be seen, but never heard; and yet, I hear them now, whispering my name like some boogeyman.

Candy Cain, Candy Cain, Candy Cain...

Their sweet eyes widen with fear as they take in my monstrous form, but I take no offense this time. I know the fear was put in their hearts long before I stepped into this church. So much scripture hammered into their skulls, like it was into mine. That's why it's so easy for me to recite a verse now from the book of Matthew as I stretch my arms wide.

"Jesus said, 'Let the children come to me, and do not hinder them.'"

It's a warning to the grownups in the pews, and the children hardly look their parents in the eye before scurrying toward the open doors and fleeing out into the daylight behind me.

"'For the kingdom of Heaven belongs to such as these.'"

Now that the innocents are out of harm's way, I can deliver my gospel to the sinners.

Heavier footsteps echo beside me as I catch an old man trying to sneak out behind the children. I grab him by his thinning hair and drag him to the basin of holy water at the center of the entryway.

"Repent!" I slam his face down in the water. "And be baptized, every one of you!"

The man's arms flail, scratching at my burned skin, peeling off slivers like the rind of an orange. The pain rings bright, my body no longer numb. Maybe this place just brings it all to the surface.

"In the name of Jesus Christ!"

The man stops scratching, starts spasming.

"For the forgiveness of your sins!"

His legs go wobbly as I press his head deeper, making sure the sacrament is complete.

"And you shall receive the gift of the Holy Spirit!"

Whatever spirit was in this man is gone now. I toss his limp body against the church doors, slamming them closed and starting the barricade.

As chaos erupts and the screaming begins, most people are running away.

But a screeching blonde woman comes at me, fists flying.

I swing my axe low, chopping into her ankle. Her foot tumbles away as she stumbles forward, collapsing on top of the first body at the door. The woman screams until I plant the axe in the back of her head, splitting it like a watermelon.

A black-haired man front-tackles me, but I hold the axe up against his chest so when we hit the ground, it crunches right through his ribcage. These sheep aren't very smart. I roll his body on top of the other two, making a fleshy pile at the doors. That should be enough to prevent any escapes, or at least slow them down long enough for me to catch them.

I turn back toward the pews, blood dripping from the axe down to my toes as Isaiah's words come to mind next.

"Now what will you do in the day of punishment? To whom will you flee for help?"

Stalking down the aisle, I wait for the next sinner to present themselves. An object is hurled at my head, and I drop the axe to catch it.

A Bible. Who throws a Bible?

Clearly the woman who's thumping her fists against my chest now. I grab her by her blouse with one hand and smack the thick book across her face, back and forth, until the light brown leather goes dark red.

The woman opens her mouth to scream, and I shove the Bible between her teeth, yanking down hard. Her jaw snaps open, hanging like a broken hinge as her tongue flaps wildly. I wrap my fingers around the slippery thing and kick her in the chest, ripping the fleshy tentacle out as her body collapses between the pews.

"Pray for me." I toss her useless tongue at her.

Two arms wrap around me from behind, and the bloody Bible falls from my grip.

"Be gone, demon!" a man shouts in my ear.

I reach back and wrap my hands around his head.

"Be seated." With one great tug, I flip the man over my shoulder and slam his spine down against the back of a pew with an audible *crack*.

The axe is back in my hands just in time to hear footsteps sprinting toward me. I make a full-bodied spin toward my next attacker, aiming the blade for her neck. It doesn't slice all the way through but turns her into a PEZ dispenser as her head flops back between her shoulder blades. Instead of candy, it's a geyser of red erupting from the stump before she collapses.

I'm trying to catch my breath when a hand slams down on my shoulder, and I swing the pick-end of the axe backwards, planting the sharp point in the grabber's face. A blind shoulder-shove pushes the body off my axe, and I turn to see the man grasping at his punctured face. The axe point caved in the space between his eyes, squishing them together as he stumbles back toward the stained-glass window. He goes crashing through the hellfire imagery as colorful shards of glass rain down.

I flip back on my heels, ready for my next attacker, but the rest of the congregation is not so bold. No more challengers, only cowards crouched beneath pews and hiding in corners. They've given up on fighting or escaping, resorting instead to prayer. Wasting their final breaths.

I visit each one like the ghost of Christmas past,

hacking my way through joint and limb as their blood baptizes my crisp skin.

I am blessed, I am healed, and as I get closer to the pulpit. . .

I see him.

His beard's a bit greyer, but I could never forget those sunken eyes.

Pastor Wendell.

My jaw clenches, until I recognize who's with him.

The three children who were in my home.

A door behind the altar opens and someone pulls them all through to the other side.

Let them run. None shall escape my judgment.

But what are those children doing here? Are they members of the congregation?

No matter. It's not for me to decide who's naughty or nice, who lives and who dies.

As I look back at the blood-soaked battlefield of the church, I'm reminded of a lesson from Bible school. A story from the crusades.

"What shall we do," a soldier asked his leader, "for we cannot distinguish between the faithful and the heretics?"

The answer was simple.

Kill them all, and let God sort them out.

CHAPTER NINE

When Fiona locks eyes with Candy Cain from across the church, she knows Abby isn't there anymore. Any hope for that girl's salvation was burned away in the fire that Fiona started. The fire that charred Candy Cain's skin and birthed the scaly beast now stalking down the church aisle.

This axe-wielding goblin is pure vengeance incarnate, ruthlessly hacking her way through the congregation like they're a swarm of enemies in World of Warcraft. Only instead of the virtual *clinks* and *clanks* of a computer game, Fiona's ears are filled with the wet squelching and panicked screaming of a real-life massacre. She knows they need to move, but they're all frozen there on the altar until a man shouts behind them.

"This way!" He has the muscled build of an orc beneath his apron as he props the door open. "Hurry!"

The cook ushers Pastor Wendell through the door first, along with a blonde teenaged boy in clerical robes and a tall woman with a tight black hair bun. Fiona follows with Austin and Mateo, and the cook locks the door behind them. She quickly surveys the kitchen, just a cold chrome box with no windows.

The blonde boy turns to the cook. "Thank God for you, Nash."

"Don't thank me yet, Timothy." Nash hurries to a metal door on the other side of the room. It won't budge, even after he throws his sizable shoulder into it. "Snow must've frozen on the other side. Knew I should've cleared it, but I got so wrapped up in meal prep."

He grabs a tin coffee mug from the counter and hurls it at the hanging pots and pans, rattling them along with Fiona's nerves. Dude's got some anger issues.

Pastor Wendell stares back at the door to the church with a haunted look in his eye. "That wasn't. . ." He sinks onto a stool at the center island. "That couldn't be. . ."

Timothy hurries to Wendell's side, putting a hand on the old man's shoulder. "That was a demon, wasn't it, Pastor?"

"That was Candy Cain," Fiona says, frustrated. "Do we have to write it in a gospel to get it through your thick skulls?"

"Hey!" Hairbun points a finger in Fiona's face. "You watch your tongue, young lady!"

"Eat it, old lady," Fiona spits back, and the old lady gasps.

"I'm thirty-six," she mutters before Pastor Wendell refocuses the conversation.

"But Candace Thornton is dead."

"You're right," Austin replies. "That was Abby."

"Abigail?" The pastor squints. "Yes, of course. The second witness."

"Witness of what?" Austin asks, but the pastor goes silent.

Fiona's more focused on the only one who's proving himself useful so far. "Nash, right?"

"Right."

"I'm Fiona." She motions to the freezer. "You got any bags of frozen veggies in there?"

"Sure, yeah. But I don't think cold corn's gonna stop that thing out there."

Fiona's knees are blazing as she hops up onto the center island, its whole surface one big wooden cutting board. "It's not for her. It's for me."

Nash digs into the freezer and brings out two bags of frozen corn. Fiona slaps them on her knees and feels the instant relief.

"Tape?" she asks.

He digs into a drawer and emerges with a roll of duct tape. "Can I help?" he asks.

"Sure." She holds the bags in place as he wraps the tape around her knees. It's a temporary fix for the inflammation, but she needs something, anything to help. When the arthritis flares, it's hard to think straight, and she really needs to think straight.

"War wounds?" Nash asks.

"Bum luck," Fiona responds.

"We need to arm ourselves," he says. "The enemy won't stop until we're dead."

"My thoughts exactly. You military?"

Nash nods, looking off. "I was, yeah. Saw some action in Desert Storm, before I found Jesus."

Fiona takes some much-needed comfort in that. Not

that Nash found Jesus, but that they've got a trained soldier on their side this time.

This time.

She can't believe she's already normalizing this nightmare that won't seem to end. But it's better to imagine herself in some slasher sequel than it is to let the horrific reality sink in and send her spinning.

Like it's spinning Mateo right now. He's just pacing in circles around the kitchen island, saying, "I can't believe this is happening again. This can't be happening again."

"I know." Austin flounders, trying to comfort his new boyfriend. "I know."

Comforting others is not her brother's strong suit. Fiona wishes she could give him some pointers, but she just needs a moment to rest, to let the cold sink into her knee joints. Just a little relief because she knows what's coming for them, and it's relentless.

At least Mateo is a step ahead of Pastor Wendell, who's stuck reciting Bible verses like a tape on repeat. "And I will appoint my two witnesses. . . And they will prophesy for 1,260 days, clothed in sackcloth. . . If anyone tries to harm them, fire comes from their mouths and devours their enem—"

Hairbun slaps him across his face, cutting his babbling short. "Get it together, Pastor!"

"Jesus, Heidi!" Wendell touches his face, eyes wide in surprise as he's finally shaken back to earth.

"Revelation won't help us," she says. "We need to move, upstairs to my classroom."

So Hairbun Heidi is the Bible school teacher. That

explains how charming she is. Still, her call to keep moving is a valid one.

"We shouldn't be here." Mateo's found a new catch phrase. "We shouldn't be here."

"I know," Austin responds once again. His empty non-assurances are annoying Fiona, so they've got to be annoying Mateo.

"No, you don't!" Mateo shouts because yep, he's definitely annoyed. "You don't know and you don't care because if you did, you wouldn't have dragged me here, Austin."

"I'm sorry," is all Austin can say in response.

"You're sorry?"

Fiona knows that tone, feels the familiar tension. It's the last thing they need right now, but after years of watching her parents, she knows the start of a couples fight when she sees one.

CHAPTER TEN

I know I shouldn't let them all get a head start, but Jesus is staring down at me from the big cross, and we have some catching up to do. I've never had a chance to see him up close, so I shimmy up the crucifix, wrap my arms around his neck and look into his eyes. They're so sad and full of pain, yet Pastor Wendell had painted this figure as someone to fear. He said that Jesus suffered for my sins, but I'm only just getting started.

I lean close to plant a kiss on his wooden cheek, and he whimpers in my ear.

Is Jesus afraid of little old me?

When I hear another whimper, I realize it's not coming from him.

It's coming from the left side of the altar. From up here, I can see over the top of the organ, where a familiar head of fake brown hair is hiding.

I hop down from the cross and circle around the organ to find a grown man curled into a ball, hands covering his ears with eyes squeezed closed.

This is the organist, and his name is. . . Isaac. How could I forget my piano teacher?

Mother made me take lessons from him, saying it would be a good source of discipline. I always found the man creepy. Like a skeleton wearing a wig.

Isaac would make me sit on this very stool as he stood behind me, putting his bony hands on my shoulders while I played. Whenever I made an error, he would squeeze. Soft pressure for the little tempo slips, but God forbid I hit a wrong note. Then his pointed fingers would pinch, only ensuring another error, until he finally commanded:

"Again, from the beginning. Music is an offering to the Lord, and every note must be pitch perfect."

The only saving grace about him standing behind me during those sessions was that I didn't have to look at his awful face the whole time. That face is looking up at me now as he reaches up to touch my hair. I flinch, but let him wipe a smudge of dark grime away to see the blonde beneath. I want him to know exactly who's come for him.

"You're not Candace. You're Abby." He smiles a crooked smile. "Sweet Abby."

Isaac seems relieved. He shouldn't be.

I open the piano stool, where all the sheet music is stored. Flipping through pages upon pages, searching until I find Isaac's favorite.

Alas! And Did My Savior Bleed

I spread the pages out on the stand, then reach my hand down toward the organist. He hesitates before taking it and rises to his feet.

The big lump in his throat moves up and down as he swallows hard. "You want me to play?"

I nod.

Isaac lowers onto the stool, and I stand behind him, wrapping my fingers around his shoulders.

He starts to play the familiar tune, and I sing, just like he taught me. Deep from my diaphragm.

"Alas! And did my Savior bleed, and did my Sovereign die!

Would He devote that sacred head for such a worm as I?"

Isaac's shaky hands fall behind the tempo of my singing, and I squeeze. My overgrown nails dig through his crisp white shirt into his flesh.

He cries out, but Isaac knows the rules, and he can't stop playing now.

I look back at Jesus on the cross as I sing.

"Was it for crimes that I have done, He groaned upon a tree?

Amazing pity! Grace unknown! And love beyond degree!"

Isaac's long fingers fumble over the G-sharp key, and I squeeze harder. His blood oozes under my fingernails.

"Well might the sun in darkness hide, and shut His glories in,

When Christ the mighty Maker died for man the creature's sin!"

He stumbles, I squeeze, he squeals and stops playing.

The organist hangs his head as he rests his hands on the keys.

"Please. . . No more. . ."

I nod in agreement, reaching over his shoulders toward the key cover. "No more. . ."

The heavy wood slams down on Isaac's frail fingers.

Bones snap as he howls, pulling his broken hands back against his chest and hunching over.

The melody is gone, but that won't stop me from singing.

"Thus might I hide my blushing face while His dear cross appears;

Dissolve my heart in thankfulness and melt mine eyes to tears."

Tears stream down Isaac's face and blood drips down his shoulders as he holds his hands out in front of his eyes. Shattered fingers all bent askew with white bone piercing through pink flesh. He'll never play piano again.

I reach for a brass pipe on the organ and wrench it loose, revealing a jagged metal point at the bottom. Gripping the pipe in my right hand, I put my left palm to Isaac's weeping face.

"But drops of tears can ne'er repay the debt of love I owe..."

His Adam's apple pulses. It was Isaac who taught me that it protects your voice box, and it was named after the fruit that Adam ate from the tree of knowledge. God made that apple stay stuck in man's throat forever as punishment for this original sin.

Isaac opens his blubbering mouth now to ask forgiveness for his own sins. "I'm sorry, Abby. I only wanted to give you the gift of music."

His gift stuck with me, but Isaac's words are hollow like the organ pipe clutched tightly in my right hand.

"Here, Lord, I give myself away..."

I tilt his head back, watch him gulp until his Adam's

apple settles. A swift stab sends the pointed pipe straight through that fleshy lump, lodging it in his voice box.

"...'tis all that I can do."

Isaac gasps, but his last breaths don't come out of his mouth. They wheeze through the pipe, sending wet death notes into the air. He's not in perfect pitch, but it's the loveliest music I've ever heard. Isaac collapses forward on the organ with a *thrum* that echoes as blood leaks out over ivory keys.

I turn back to Jesus on the cross to ask over the chaotic sound.

"My God, why would You shed Your blood, so pure and undefiled

To make a sinful one like me, Your chosen, precious child?"

He doesn't answer with words, but the music dies and the church goes quiet.

Quiet enough for me to hear the voices shouting in the next room.

This is my calling.

I've been summoned to silence them all.

CHAPTER ELEVEN

Mateo can't stop his voice from booming. "We should be safe and sound at the hospital right now!"

He's never been more mad at his best friend, his new boyfriend. It was pretty bold of Austin to stake that claim in front of the whole congregation, and it's not like the new couple had time to set the relationship status on their AIM profiles while running nonstop from a psycho killer, but Mateo is having all kinds of regrets now.

"I'm sorry," Austin says. If he says 'I know' or 'I'm sorry' one more time, Mateo might slap him harder than Heidi just slapped Pastor Wendell.

"Sorry isn't good enough," Mateo says. "Sorry doesn't get us out of here alive."

"How was I supposed to know she'd come back?"

"Evil finds a way," Pastor Wendell mumbles.

Mateo rolls his eyes, stays focused on Austin. "This isn't about Candy Cain. It's about you and your self-righteous mission to shame some strangers and heal your daddy issues."

Austin looks genuinely hurt as he crosses his arms in a defensive posture. "Too soon, man."

"Guys. . ." Fiona tries to interject, but Mateo's not hearing it.

"Valerie was right," he says. "We should have never left LA in the first place." Mateo's thinking of his parents and his little brother Leo back home. What if he never gets to see them again?

"Maybe you're right." Austin shrugs. "If you hadn't come from LA, we never would've found that video, and my dad never would've brought it to the sheriff and gotten killed."

Mateo's rage-meter clicks up from mad to pissed. "So now it's all *my* fault?"

"I'm just saying, we would've—"

"You would've been murdered in your sleep!"

"You don't know tha—"

"Hey!" Fiona shouts, hopping down from the counter with a visible wince. "I am not about to get caught between two feuding parents again, so you both better put this stupid fight on pause until we get out of here alive. Got me?"

Fiona's right. Fiona's always right. Mateo takes a deep breath, calming himself. "Fine. Can we just find a way to—"

THWACK!

The bloody axe blade splinters through the wooden door.

"O come, all ye faithful!"

Mateo shivers at her voice. Not the singing again, please, anything but the singing.

"Joyful and triumphant!"

Heidi claps twice, going into full teacher mode. "Okay, listen up. We've got two choices." She raises her voice above the singing and the chopping. "Either we stay here and fight, or we keep moving upstairs."

"O come ye, O come ye to Bethlehem!"

"I vote for option three," Nash says, rolling up the sleeves on his tree-trunk forearms. "You all head upstairs. Barricade that door until you get the verbal 'all clear' from me. I'll handle the little girl myself."

The axe is making quick work of that door. Mateo flashes back to the moment he hacked through that bathroom door and watched Candy Cain tear Valerie apart. He can't stand to see any more bloodshed today.

"Come, and behold Him!"

Fiona grabs Nash by his muscled arm. "You should come with us. We're gonna need you."

"Born the King of angels!"

Nash shakes his head. "This is my kitchen."

"O come, let us adore Him!"

"I will defend it from all enemies." He glares through the hole in the door as Candy Cain flashes a grin on the other side. "Both foreign and domestic."

"O come, let us adore Him!"

A blackened hand bursts through the kitchen door, pawing at the lock.

"O come, let us adore Him!"

"Go on!" Nash yells to the group. "Get out of here!"

Mateo leads the scramble toward the door on the other side of the kitchen as Nash announces behind them. "The enemy has breached!"

"Christ, the Lord!"

CHAPTER TWELVE

My arms are already sore after swinging the axe through all that flesh and bone in the church, so hacking my way through the kitchen door now is extra tiring. Marjorie's brain stew was a nutritious snack, but my energy is sapped by the time I finally unlock the door and enter the kitchen.

When I do, the cook is waiting. Nash looks even more muscly than I remember as he sharpens his meat cleaver against the metal rod, arms bulging.

"Hello, little girl," he says without even looking me in the eye. "I hear you've been very naughty this year."

I grit my teeth as a memory boils up in my brain.

When Mother and Father put Candace in her Bad Girl Box, sometimes they wouldn't even feed her. After Marjorie's complaints, they withheld food for days while Candace stayed trapped in the cramped dark. I snuck down into the cellar and sung songs through the hatch door to keep her company, but I knew that wasn't enough. Her weak voice was barely loud enough to reach my ears through the wood.

"Hungry."

I had to help my sister.

Mother kept a strict inventory, so I couldn't sneak food from the house. That's why I slipped away from Bible school the next day and into the church kitchen. I started stuffing canned food from the lower cabinet into my backpack, but before I could zip it up, a hand clamped down on my wrist, lifting me off my feet.

"You little thief," Nash growled.

I thought my arm was going to pop loose from my shoulder as he dragged me over to the island.

"You know what they do to thieves over in Iraq?" He pressed my hand to the cutting board top and pulled the meat cleaver from the block of knives. "They chop your hand off, right here at the wrist." Nash pressed the sharp blade against my skin, hard enough to hurt, but soft enough to not break skin. Then he raised the blade high.

"Forgive me!" I cried.

"I'm not the one you need forgiveness from."

Nash swung the cleaver down. The blade stuck into the board so close to my fingers, I felt a little gust come off the cold steel.

"You best be thankful you're being raised in a good Christian community." He dragged me to the back door.

Outside, Pastor Wendell was tending to his garden, pulling rocks from the soil and collecting them in a bucket.

"Sorry to disturb you, Pastor," Nash announced. "But I caught this one stealing food in the kitchen."

Pastor Wendell stood up and dusted the dirt from his knees. "Abigail Thornton. I fear your sister's wicked ways are rubbing off on you." He lifted the bucket of rocks and walked over. "Do you know why I have to pull the rocks from the soil?" He loved asking questions, but never waited for an answer. "Much like sin, they disrupt healthy growth. That's why I must hunt them down and rip them out by force. For the good of the garden."

Wendell bent down to face me, breath reeking of alcohol. "Proverbs 20:17. Food gained by fraud tastes sweet. But one ends up with a mouth full of gravel."

He held the bucket out to Nash with a nod. The cook scooped a handful of loose stones and shoved them in my mouth. They scraped against my teeth, crowding in against my tongue as the former soldier commanded: "Swallow."

And I did.

It occurs to me now, staring at Nash ten years later, that those rocks never did make their way out of my body. They must still be stuck in my belly, the core of my insides all hardened around foreign stone.

Nash raises his meat cleaver high. "You owe me a hand."

I raise my right hand and wiggle all my fingers, daring him to come get them.

The veins bulge in Nash's neck as he charges across the kitchen. I swing my axe up into the hanging pot holder above, using the leverage to propel myself feet-first and dropkick him in the chest. His heavy body falls back to the floor between the stove and the island.

With the axe stuck up in the pot holder, I reach for the block of knives on top of the island. Before I can pull one, Nash leaps to his feet and grabs me by the neck with an iron grip, squeezing the breath out of me. He presses my cheek against the stove burner.

"A simmer for a sinner." He flips the burner on low.

The blue flame sparks alive, singeing my already scorched face.

My skin bubbles and bursts, but I feel no pain.

The fire can't hurt me anymore.

It's inside me now.

My hand reaches across on the counter, grasping at a meat tenderizer, and I swing the metal mallet against the side of Nash's skull. He stumbles back against the island, slipping down to a forced seat when his legs kick out in front of him.

There's a dazed look in his eyes as blood seeps from the patterned head wound above his ear. When he reaches a hand up, I bend it back to the cutting board surface behind him. Grabbing a kitchen knife, I slam it through his palm like an iron nail.

Nash screams, reaching his other hand up toward the pinned one, but I intercept it, stretch it wide with a *pop* of his shoulder and put another knife through that hand.

The crucifixion is complete.

His eyes roll around in his head, brain buzzing from blunt-force trauma as he looks up toward the ceiling and quotes Christ on the cross. "Father, into your hands I commend my spirit."

I shake my head. He's looking in the wrong direction. I tilt his face down toward the floor and the inferno that awaits him below.

The stove burner is still on *Low* as I fill a small pot with water, set it atop the flame and crank it up to *High*.

Bending down to the lower cupboard, I pull a can of baked beans and hold it in front of Nash's googly eyes, quoting a Bible verse.

"If your enemy is hungry, feed him. . ."

I punch the can against his teeth. It takes several slams to knock most of the front ones out as bloody Chiclets blubber down his chin. Reaching for a can opener, I crank it against the aluminum until the top pops off. I run a finger along the can's edge, so sharp it slices my skin right open.

With no teeth in the way, it's much easier to shove the can into Nash's mouth, scraping over his gums until it hits the back of his throat.

"Swallow," I command, and he does.

Coughing and gagging, he takes big gulps of the beans until I can feel the can is empty. But I don't want him to spit it out, so I give the can a few quick twists. Nash releases a muffled howl as the serrated aluminum slices beneath his tongue, screwing deep into the flesh at the back of his throat. I release my grip, and the can stays in place as his head rolls back, barely conscious now. I don't want him to miss the next part, so I better hurry.

The small pot of water is already boiling on the stove as I grip it by the plastic handle. "If he is thirsty, give him something to drink."

I press the hot pot against Nash's lips and tilt it back, pouring the boiling water into the cook's crowded mouth. It sizzles against the aluminum, and I can see his fleshy throat swelling, hugging tighter around the can until his gagging and gurgling stops because no more air can escape.

Nash's fingers twitch against the knives that pin his hands in place until his whole body goes limp. I look up toward a God I no longer believe in, finishing Nash's crucifixion quote with a slight adjustment, just in case.

"Father, don't forgive them. For they know exactly what they do."

I pull the knives from Nash's palms, releasing his corpse. There will be no hero's burial. After the crucifixion comes the resurrection.

CHAPTER THIRTEEN

A classroom during winter break is the last place Austin wants to be, but that's exactly where he and the others find themselves now. All the desks are in perfect alignment as he rushes down the aisle toward the wall of windows in search of a potential escape route.

"Come, Pastor Wendell," Timothy says, guiding his mentor to one of the desks. "Rest."

The shellshocked pastor takes a seat. "Do you think Nash will be okay?"

"He can handle himself," Heidi says.

Mateo shakes his head. "You've clearly never met Candy Cain."

Austin pops a rectangular awning window open, but it only creates two feet of space for someone to crawl through. It's a tight squeeze, and when he sticks his head through the gap, he sees the larger problem. The iced-over garden below is a good thirty feet away. No way anybody's walking away from that leap of faith.

"Window's not gonna work." He turns to Heidi. "Is there a phone in here?"

"A phone?" she scoffs. "What kind of classroom do you think I'm running here?"

"A real fun one." Mateo points to a banner above the chalkboard.

Whoever loves discipline loves knowledge, but whoever hates correction is stupid. Proverbs 12:1

Fiona points at the student essays taped to the wall, all of them marked with red F's. "Since when are there grades in Bible school?"

"God keeps score," Heidi replies, "and so do I. Children need to be reminded that they can always be better."

"No wonder all those kids ran for their lives." Fiona turns away from Heidi and approaches Austin at the window. "Hey. Might wanna try this." She digs into her pocket, pulling out a square black cellular phone with a full keyboard. "Merry Christmas."

Austin blinks hard. "Is that my Blackberry?"

"I grabbed it while Sheriff Brock was getting torched," she explains, "but there was no service back at the house, so I didn't bother mentioning it. I honestly forgot I had it until you mentioned a phone."

Austin smiles at his sister. "I can't believe you stole my Christmas present."

Fiona shrugs. "Don't tell Santa."

Pastor Wendell is still catching up at his desk. "Sheriff Brock is... dead?"

"Oh yeah," Mateo replies. "Like six ways from Sunday, dude."

Fiona shows the lit-up Blackberry screen to Austin. "Looks like Dad already set it up and charged it for you."

"Of course he did." When it came to technology, his father's attention to detail was always on point. Not so much in other arenas.

Austin looks at the service bar, singular. He punches in 9-1-1 and presses *Send*, but the screen immediately says *Call Failed*. "It's not going through. I need more service."

Wendell shakes his head. "Nothing gets through this old stone structure."

Austin holds the Blackberry out the window as far as he can reach, careful not to drop it. "Come on, come on."

A second bar flickers in and out, taunting him, but every time he presses *Send*, the same rejection fills the screen.

Call Failed.

It feels personal, like God is rubbing it in his face.

The screen might as well say: *Austin Failed.*

"The service might be better up in the rectory," Timothy offers. "Nearer to God."

"Cool tip, Tim." Fiona leans over Austin's shoulder. "Check to see if there's some kind of override to get an emergency call out."

Austin searches through the applications on the screen, looking for any symbol that remotely resembles an emergency. He can't find anything like that, but he does come across a little icon that says *Notes* with the number *1*.

He clicks it and reads:

Austin,

We're so proud of the young man you've become. No

matter how old you get or how far from home life takes you, never forget that family is only a phone call away.

Love,

Mom & Dad

Austin's legs turn to instant Jell-O, and he collapses, arms latching onto a desk that clatters to the floor beside him.

In the momentary blackout, he hears Mateo cry out "Austin!" and then his boyfriend is by his side on the classroom floor.

"What is it?" Fiona asks.

Austin can't speak as he hands his sister the phone. She reads the message and tears up, handing it to Mateo so she can hug her brother.

After reading the note, Mateo takes Austin's hand. "I'm so sorry. For what I said earlier."

"It doesn't matter." He's too numb to feel the warmth of Mateo's touch. "I just want this to be over."

Heidi's harsh voice comes in response. "Then you need to toughen up, all of you. We don't have time for all your little feelings."

Austin looks up into the eyes of the cruel woman. He might not know Heidi very well, but he knows enough to hate her. "I don't think you understand what we've been through tonight."

"Yes, yes, you told us. Your parents were killed, and that's all very sad, but it was clearly God's will."

"Heidi." Wendell shakes his head. "Please."

"Do you disagree, Pastor?" When he doesn't respond, she just keeps running her mouth. "They brought their reckoning to our door, but we need not suffer for their sins."

And with that, Austin knows *more* than enough to hate her. "What about *your* sins?" He gets to his feet, rage conquering the numbness. "You know damn well this didn't start with us."

Wendell leaps from his chair. "It started with the Devil!"

Fiona rolls her eyes. "God, you are such a cliché. It's all 'Devil this' and 'evil that.'"

Wendell raises a finger. "You have no idea what we're dealing with. I witnessed the evolution of this corruption firsthand."

Austin squints at the crazy cleric. "What evolution? What are you talking about?"

Heidi crosses her arms. "We don't have time to educate you ignorant children."

"This isn't education." Fiona motions to the classroom. "It's indoctrination."

"Enough!" Heidi raises an open palm, ready to strike Fiona, but Austin's quick to grab her by the wrist.

"Touch my sister and I'll take your ass to school."

The threat sounded cool in his head, but he can see Mateo stifling a laugh.

Still, it makes Heidi all flustered as she pulls away from his grip. "This is *my* classroom, and I will not stand for—"

THUMP-THUMP.

Someone's knocking on the door. Through the warped glass, Nash's unmistakably large stature is visible.

"He did it." Heidi lurches for the door.

Fiona shakes her head. "Nash said not to open it without a verbal—"

"I've had enough verbal out of you!" Heidi shouts over her shoulder as she unlocks the door and swings it open. "Is she dead?"

It's going to be hard for Nash to answer with that aluminum can jammed down his throat. Heidi screams as the cook's corpse falls forward, toppling her to the floor and revealing Candy Cain behind him.

The prodigal student returned.

CHAPTER FOURTEEN

"Proverbs 1:7," Miss Heidi commanded.

I stood next to Candace at the blackboard, chalk in hand, while our teacher hovered behind us, casting her tall shadow on the dark green slate. I knew my sister could never retrieve a Bible quote on command, so I was trying hard to remember the verse for both our sakes.

Before I could summon the words, I heard the *thwack* and saw Candace spasm from the strike of Miss Heidi's beloved ruler.

"Proverbs!" she barked. "1:7!"

The verse suddenly came to me, a saving grace. "Fear of the Lord is the beginning of knowledge!"

Miss Heidi nodded. "Very good, Abby. Now write it."

I started scrawling the words on the blackboard.

"Both of you."

Candace stared blank-eyed until I gave her a nudge. We both dragged the chalk along the board, my words swooping in perfect cursive while Candace etched harsh lines that connected into misshapen letters. By the time I finished writing the verse, Candace had only just completed the word FEAR.

"Candace," Miss Heidi said. "I fear you simply aren't listening to my teachings. If you can't hear me then you cannot hear the Lord." When Candace didn't respond, Miss Heidi tugged her ear and leaned down to yell. "Can you hear me?!"

Candace was visibly biting her tongue when I interjected, trying to distract the woman. "Miss Heidi, I have a question."

The teacher released her grip on my sister's ear, wiping her fingers on her dress. "What is your question, Abby?"

"You and Pastor Wendell talk a lot about fear. But isn't God love?" As much as it was a diversion, I really did want to know the answer.

"Oh, child." Miss Heidi bent down, her voice going honey sweet. "Fear is the heart of love."

Even at eight years old, I knew in my heart of hearts that this was wrong. There was something rotten in Nodland, but I was still just a child. There was nowhere to go, nowhere to hide from God in this town. I dreamed of someday escaping with Candace, starting life anew with my sister, but every dream died in this old church.

"Did I say you could stop?" Miss Heidi asked Candace with another *thwack* of the ruler across her backside.

"What about Matthew?" I blurted, anything to distract as Candace picked up the chalk again.

"What about him?" Miss Heidi asked.

"Didn't he say something about not fearing those who kill the body?"

Miss Heidi grinned. "Very good memory, Abby. Matthew 10:28. 'Do not fear those who kill the body but cannot kill the soul. Rather fear the one who can destroy both soul and body in hell.' Do you know who that one is?"

I nodded. "It's the—"

SCREEEEEECH!

Candace dragged her fingernails down the chalkboard.

"Devil!" Miss Heidi shrieked as she reared back her ruler and *thwacked* it against Candace's hand, drawing blood. "I will teach you to disrespect my blackboard!"

Thwack! against her other hand.

Desperate to stop the assault on my sister, I grabbed the chalk and wrote one big word above Candace's boxy letters to spell out our collective prayer.

Miss Heidi gasped at my sin. "Abigail. Not *you*."

I looked at my sister, whimpering as she held her bloodied hands against her chest. Then I shot daggers straight into Miss Heidi's eyes with a defiant grin. "And fuck you, too."

The ruler nearly broke against my cheek, leaving a bruise for days that Mother and Father never questioned.

Standing at the classroom threshold now, I rub my jaw at the phantom pain.

The sound of scurrying draws my attention to the far side of the classroom, where Pastor Wendell and the others are already disappearing through the next door. I'll catch them when class is dismissed.

Miss Heidi trembles on the floor beneath the dead cook as I step over her and head for the teacher's desk. Opening the drawer, I find her beloved ruler there. The same one from ten years ago.

Miss Heidi rolls Nash's corpse away and gets to her feet, trying to flee when I *thwack* the sturdy wood against the back of her leg, dropping her to all fours. I use the ruler like a herding tool, *thwacking* her arms and legs, steering my cattle toward the chalkboard.

A swift upper hand hit to Miss Heidi's rear end makes the schoolteacher leap to her feet.

"What do you want from me, Devil?" she asks.

"Jeremiah. 6:11."

Miss Heidi reaches for the chalk, but it trembles in her hand. "I don't..."

Thwack goes the ruler against her right ear.

"Jeremiah!" *Thwack* to the left ear. "6:11!"

Miss Heidi clutches her ears as she cries out. "I don't remember!"

I grab the hypocritical teacher by her tightly knotted hair bun and ram her face against the chalkboard. Once, twice, three times before spinning her on her feet.

"Jeremiah 6:11." I watch the blood run down Miss Heidi's busted nose into her mouth as I recite it myself. "But I am full of the wrath of the Lord."

Placing the ruler on the chalkboard ledge, I take a

long piece of chalk in each hand and stretch my arms wide.

"I am weary of holding it in."

My fists arc forward in a wrathful swing, jamming the chalk into Miss Heidi's ears.

Can she hear the Lord now?

The teacher howls as I grab the eraser from the ledge and slam it against her mouth, sending puffs of chalk dust down her lungs. Miss Heidi coughs and gurgles, blood gushing from every hole.

I snap the ruler against the chalkboard ledge, splintering wood into a jagged point. I hope her ears still work so she can hear her favorite verse from my lips.

"Those who spare the rod. . ."

Miss Heidi's eyes are wide in fear, and I wonder if she feels loved in this moment.

". . .hate their children."

The sharpened ruler jabs up under her chin, piercing through soft flesh and pinning her tongue to the roof of her mouth. With no more scripture to spout, Miss Heidi's useless body slides down the chalkboard, slumping to a seat on the ground.

I pluck a piece of bloodied chalk from her ear and scrawl a message on the blackboard in white and red. I'm the teacher now with a lesson for all of Nodland.

CANDY CAIN
SAVES

CHAPTER FIFTEEN

I f Fiona has to climb one more set of stairs, she really is going to burn this whole church to the ground. When the group enters the rectory, she finds an ornate chair that looks more like a throne and sits to rest her knees. Hanging on the wall beside her is a big painting of Pastor Wendell with a saintly halo around his head. Yikes, what an ego.

"We shouldn't have left Heidi like that," Timothy says, locking the door behind them.

"I tried to educate her." Fiona doesn't feel bad about leaving that nasty Bible school teacher behind. She doesn't even feel bad about not feeling bad.

"Barely another bar," Austin says, already moving around the small room, holding the Blackberry up to different corners while clicking wildly on every button. "And the battery is draining quick."

Pastor Wendell reaches out a hand. "Give it here. I may know a little trick."

Austin hands him the device, and Wendell takes it toward an old wooden door, holding it up against the cracks. "Almost."

He creaks the door open, letting a gust of cold air into the room.

Fiona shivers. "What's in there?"

"The belfry stairs." He takes a step through the door onto the first stair. "Now, if I can just. . ." The pastor darts through the door and slams it behind him. The metal *clunk* that comes next sounds a whole lot like a lock being engaged.

"Pastor?" Timothy hurries to the door and gives it a useless tug, confirming exactly what Fiona suspected.

"What a scumbag." She shakes her head, annoyed but not surprised.

"No." Timothy places a hand on the door. "No, he's just going up in the belfry to call for help, that's all."

"Sure," Mateo says, "and until help arrives, he's got us sacrificial lambs to slow her down."

Austin is still staring at his empty hand where the phone just was. "I can't believe I just fell for that."

"Don't beat yourself up," Fiona says, even though she can't believe he just fell for that either. But there's no sense dwelling on it as she stands up and gets in Timothy's face. "You know this room, right? This is where you and Pastor Asshole get all dressed up for your performative nonsense?"

"This is where the holy father and I prepare the sacraments for sacred service."

"That's what I said. Any weapons in here?"

"It's a rectory, not an armory. There's nothing here but ceremonial artifacts." Timothy motions to a small altar in the corner.

"Well, even ceremonial artifacts can bust skulls."

Fiona makes her way over and starts browsing the weird collection of religious trinkets. She finds a metal ball attached to a chain and starts swinging it. "Is this a mace?"

"It's a thurible." Timothy snatches it from her and places it back on the altar. "You fill it with incense to bless the church."

Fiona shrugs. The ball was too light to do any real damage anyway, but she spots her weapon of choice leaning against the altar. A long silver staff, topped with a crucifix. Now she's got a second cane *and* a weapon. Praise the Lord.

"What's in here?" Mateo opens a large armoire and starts pushing aside all the robes.

"Don't touch those!" Timothy cries. "Pastor Wendell likes his robes cleaned every Sunday, and your dirty little hands—"

"Hey!" Austin grabs Timothy by the shoulders. "Keep up, altar boy. Your holy father just dropped you like a bad habit. He doesn't care about you."

"No, no, no." Timothy covers his ears, refusing to hear, to believe.

Fiona can't help feeling a little bad for the kid. But not a lot bad.

Mateo shrugs at the hanging robes. "Nothing but a bunch of tacky dresses."

"Wait." Something catches Fiona's eye through the clothing. She squats, leaning into the armoire to inspect the back wall. It's a lighter-colored wood than the rest. In video games, that usually means something you can interact with, like a secret passage or a hiding place. She presses her palm against it, and the false back comes loose.

"Damn, Fiona." Mateo crouches behind her. "That's some Nancy Drew shit."

"I prefer Poirot." When she moves the light wood board, Fiona finds a secret compartment built into the stone wall.

"What do you see?" Mateo asks.

In the darkness rests an old piece of equipment Fiona doesn't recognize. It's the shape of a small briefcase with two spindles where reels would go and a set of recording buttons. "I think it's some kind of film projector?"

Mateo leans over her shoulder to inspect. "That's not a film projector. It's an old school tape recorder." He turns back to Austin. "Remember when Ethan made us watch *Evil Dead*?"

"The one where the tape summons demons that possess the friends until they all murder each other?" Austin asks. "Maybe let's not mess with this thing."

A big metal storage canister rests beside the recorder, and Fiona drags it out to read the words written on the masking tape label. "The Absolution Sessions."

She pops the latches and opens the lid, revealing a collection of reels inside. Pulling them one by one, all labeled with different names. "Elsinger. . . Turley. . . Dolbow. . ."

Her heart stops when she sees a familiar name, showing it to Mateo and Austin. "Thornton."

Mateo gets to work on threading the reel through the machine while Fiona confronts Timothy. "What are the Absolution Sessions?"

"I don't know. I swear, I've never heard those words before in my life."

"You're the youth pastor. Wendell trusts you."

Timothy shakes his head, repeating Austin's words. "He doesn't care about me." The youth pastor motions to the hidden compartment. "Why else would he hide them in there?"

The kid's got a point, but Fiona still doesn't trust him. She'll have to keep a closer eye on blondie moving forward.

Mateo finishes clicking the reel into place. "I'm not exactly an expert with this old thing, but I think I've got it threaded through."

"We sure we want to do this?" Austin asks.

"It's what we're here for, right?" Mateo's finger hovers over the *Play* button. "To get some answers?"

"I'll be on Candy Cain watch." Fiona grips the staff and turns to the door that leads down to the classroom. "Just play the damn thing."

Mateo clicks *Play* and the audio crackles to life.

A warbled voice comes through the tinny speakers on the side of the machine.

"The date is October 30th, 1995. My name is Pastor Wendell Wake. And these are the Absolution Sessions with Abigail and Candace Thornton. . ."

CHAPTER SIXTEEN

PASTOR WENDELL: Candace. Miss Heidi tells me you were being disruptive in class again. Do you want to tell me why?

CANDACE: She's a liar.

PASTOR WENDELL: So, you weren't being disruptive in class?

CANDACE: No. I was being disruptive in class because she's a liar. Everything she teaches. All lies.

PASTOR WENDELL: Miss Heidi teaches the Bible, and the Bible is truth.

ABIGAIL: I think what Candace means is—

PASTOR WENDELL: I was not addressing you, Abigail. Your sister can speak for herself. Can't you, Candace?

CANDACE: Yes. I can.

PASTOR WENDELL: Now, what is it that you believe to be untrue about Miss Heidi's teachings?

CANDACE: That God loves everyone.

PASTOR WENDELL: Is that it? You don't believe that God loves you?

CANDACE: I don't believe that God loves *you*.

PASTOR WENDELL: Well, that's not a very Christ-like thing to say, is it?

CANDACE: I never said I was Christ.

PASTOR WENDELL: Then who are you, Candace? Is this indeed Candace Thornton that I'm speaking to? Or someone, some*thing* else?

CANDACE: You're only ever speaking to yourself, Pastor.

PASTOR WENDELL: Okay. I can see that we won't be getting anywhere today. Abigail, be a good girl and tell me what happened after class today.

ABIGAIL: Miss Heidi had us write on the blackboard.

PASTOR WENDELL: And what did you write on the blackboard?

ABIGAIL: Proverbs. 1:7.

PASTOR WENDELL: Is that right? Because I've read Proverbs many times over, and I don't recall seeing the word F-U-C-K in those pages.

ABIGAIL: Maybe you're just not looking hard enough.

PASTOR WENDELL: What did you just say to me?

[pause]

PASTOR WENDELL: Abigail. I'm speaking to you.

[pause]

ABIGAIL: You're only ever speaking to yourself, Pastor.

[click]

The date is November 5th, 1995. This is
Pastor Wendell Wake. The case of Abigail
and Candace Thornton continues to be ever
more perplexing.

All of my other Absolution Sessions with
the children of Nodland have been seam-
less. I know that every child is born
with sin in their soul, but I've been
able to provoke that evil to the surface,
isolate it and remove it from each child
through my unique rite of exorcism. To
cleanse them, make them perfect in the
eyes of the Lord. This is my great
mission from God above. To pluck the
darkness at its roots before it has a
chance to blossom in a child's heart.

But the Thornton girls offer a unique chal-
lenge. It's as though whenever I think I've
removed the evil from one girl, it appears
in the other. Not two separate seeds, but
one shifting presence. I suspect that what
we're dealing with here is not original
sin, but demonic possession. Satan's spawn
is bouncing from one host to the other,
evading exorcism. According to the Bible,
the only true solution is a cleansing by
fire, but I am not so harsh in my ways. I'm
hoping it won't come to that.

I've met with the girls' parents and
encouraged them to be unerring in their
judgment. They have their own theory,
that their children are harbingers of the
apocalypse. I see no such evidence and
still believe Candace to be the true
source of this evil, the original vessel,
like Eve corrupting Adam. If this iden-
tity is reinforced, over and over again,
we might still be able to isolate and
expunge it from the child's soul. But the
more we chase it from one girl to the
other, the more powerful it grows, and
the less chance we have of containing the
evil. I can only hope it's not too late
to catch this tiger by its tail and kill
the beast for good.

[click]

The date is December 20th, 1995.

Our efforts appear to be working. The
evil seems more focused than ever within
Candace Thornton's soul.

Christmas is fast approaching and I've
just met with her parents to give them
more guidance. This sacred holiday offers
us a chance to redouble our efforts, to
ensure that we can save at least one soul

from eternal damnation. What better day
to do so than on the birthday of Christ
himself?

I advised the Thorntons to buy as many
gifts as they could for Abigail, to
shower her with love and praise. I even
gave them expressed permission to
purchase toys from the outside heathen
world, dolls and tricycles and other
earthly distractions.

For Candace, I provided them with a
special gift. I had Nash fetch a piece of
coal from the kitchen barbecue and told
the Thorntons to put it in Candace's
stocking.

I believe this will be the final nail to
pin down the evil that possesses Candace
Thornton's soul. Once the girl has fully
accepted her evil nature, they will bring
her to church for Christmas morning
service, and I will perform my rite of
exorcism that has purified so many children in Nodland.

Lesser men may have given up on such an
evil child, but I am driven by my holy
duty. I will not let one black sheep
taint the whole flock. I will shepherd

her soul towards the light, and banish
this darkness on Christmas day.
I do this in thy name, Heavenly Father.

[click]

It's December. . . December 25th, 1995.

They're dead. The whole family. Burned to
death, a cleansing by fire. I see now
that the Thorntons were right after all.
Their daughters were the two witnesses
from the Book of Revelation.

"They have the power to shut up the
heavens."

But they're gone now, as prophesied.
Killed and left unburied.

"The inhabitants of the earth will gloat
over them and will celebrate by sending
each other gifts, because these two
prophets had tormented those who live on
the earth."

And so we shall celebrate their death on
this day of gift giving.

It all makes sense now, of course. That

the two witnesses came and were killed
before my full transcendence.

It's not until the final chapters of
Revelation that my second coming is
foretold.

But I am here now, fully realized, and I
will continue in my mission to do thy
will, Father.

For I am thy son, Jesus Christ, returned
to cleanse the world of sin.

Forevermore.

CHAPTER SEVENTEEN

Mateo's fist clenches as he listens to the awful audiotape.

He didn't hear evil jumping from one sister to another. He heard two siblings protecting each other.

Like the time Mateo got in big trouble with his parents for filming an homage to *Reservoir Dogs* in the backseat of the family car. Ethan played an excellent Mr. Orange, screaming and flailing in all that fake blood while Austin's Mr. White comforted him from behind the wheel. But it turns out fake blood doesn't come out of fabric seats very easily.

Mom and Dad were pissed for days, until Leo broke the ceramic vase they'd bought while visiting abuela in Mexico. Just like that, all the anger was drawn from one brother to the other, with Mateo's sin quickly forgotten. If the heat ever got too much on Leo, Mateo would pull some other stunt to create a fresh diversion. It was never planned or plotted, but some kind of unspoken agreement between the brothers. A silent love language to keep each other safe.

When the final reel rolls out, Mateo grabs Timothy by his collar. He's tempted to tie the youth pastor to that fancy chair and Mr. Blonde him right now. "You really expect us to believe you didn't know about this?"

"I didn't, I swear to God himself!" Timothy cries.

Mateo pins Timothy up against the open armoire door, rattling wood.

"Mateo." Austin puts a hand on his shoulder. "Easy."

He shrugs Austin's hand off and shoots daggers at Timothy. "Your precious pastor was playing mad Christian scientist right here in the church, and you knew nothing?!"

Timothy doesn't shy away from Mateo's fiery gaze. "I know he saved me." His eyes are wet, words heavy. "I'm a child of Nodland too."

Mateo releases his grip, realizing that Timothy is just as brainwashed as the rest of them, if not more so. How much Kool-Aid does it take to become the right-hand man to the Kool-Aid Man himself?

Fiona's still stuck on that last bit of audio. "So, Pastor Wendell thinks he's Jesus Christ, huh? That checks out."

"I knew there was something off about that guy," Austin says. "Candy Cain is clearly here for revenge."

Mateo turns to him, eye socket throbbing from all the blood pumping into his head. "That doesn't mean she's gonna spare us."

Whatever happened in the past doesn't change the fact that Candy Cain is a monster hellbent on carving her way through anyone who gets in her way. And right now, there's nowhere for them to be but in her way.

Distant footsteps echo up toward the rectory.

Fiona's voice drops to a whisper. "What are the chances that's Miss Heidi?"

The answer comes in faraway song. *"Nearer, my God, to thee!"*

"Less than zero." Mateo tries to force the locked belfry door open, hoping he's stronger than Timothy, but the old wood is sturdier than it looks.

"Nearer to thee!" The voice grows closer.

"I have a plan," Timothy says.

Mateo shakes his head. "We don't trust you."

"Give me a chance."

"A chance for what?"

"For absolution." Timothy points to the armoire. "Get in."

"E'en though it be a cross that raiseth me. . ." Footsteps ascending.

"We'll be sitting ducks in there," Fiona says.

"Not with a sacrificial lamb out here." Timothy helps her climb inside.

Mateo and Austin exchange a helpless glance, no other options presenting themselves. They climb inside with Fiona.

"Just stay quiet," Timothy says.

". . . still all my song shall be!"

"There's room in here for four," Fiona offers.

"Nearer, my God, to thee. . ." So close now, right outside the door.

Timothy shakes his head. "If she's here for vengeance, then she's here for me."

Mateo's jaw goes slack. "You knew her?"

Timothy's lip quivers. "I loved her."

He closes the armoire doors, leaving the three of them in the dark. Mateo can't help thinking of that little box where Candy Cain had been locked away in the cellar. At least he's not alone like she was. He wraps his arms around Austin, who wraps his arms around Fiona.

"Nearer, my God, to thee. . ."

They're a tangle of trembling limbs holding tight in the dark.

The rectory door *creeeaks* open as the voice of vengeance enters the room.

"Nearer to thee!"

CHAPTER EIGHTEEN

I'm surprised to find the rectory door unlocked. This is where Pastor Wendell took me and Candace for those little chats, and he always locked the door.

But the only one here now is a boy on his knees at the corner altar. His back is to me, but I can see his blonde head bowed in prayer through the mirror above the table full of shiny junk. He's gripping the big silver crucifix around his neck, and I can hear his words more clearly as I approach.

"Forgive me, Abby." His head tilts up, giving me a clear view of the sad boy in the mirror. "For I have sinned."

My heart twists like a screw, and I clutch my chest at the sudden pain.

It's Timothy.

The boy who loved me.

The parents of Nodland encouraged their children to find partners early, to build their love around Christ until they were old enough to marry and birth more children. That's what the youth ministry was for: pairing children off and preparing them for the melding ceremony. Once melded, they would either mate here in the community or go on a mission to the outside world.

I remember the first time Timothy held my hand during Sunday service. We were only eight years old, palms sweaty with the hymnal books open on our legs as we read together. Mother and Father were so proud.

Afterwards, Timothy took me by the hand and led me up the stairs into the rectory.

"I know where Pastor Wendell keeps his special juice." He pulled a glass container of red wine from the corner altar.

"I don't think we're supposed to be up here." I rubbed my arms, scared of getting in trouble.

"Don't worry." Timothy swigged from the bottle and passed it to me. "I'll protect you."

I took a reluctant sip of the wine and winced. "Tastes bad."

"I think it's supposed to taste bad. Grownups don't like sweet things like kids do."

I wanted so badly to be a grownup, so I took a deeper gulp of wine and wiped the red from my lips.

Timothy smiled at me. "I love you, Abigail Thornton."

My heart cracked open. For the first time in my young life, I felt like anything was possible. Like my life could be so much more. "I love you, Timothy."

We would soon be melded, and I could only pray that we'd be given a mission outside of Nodland. Maybe I could even convince Pastor Wendell to let us take Candace with us, since no one wanted to meld with my sister anyway.

Timothy took the bottle from me and had another big sip before setting it aside to say: "I think we should kiss."

My face bunched up in confusion. The first kiss was meant to be the culmination of the melding ceremony in front of the congregation. "I don't think I'm ready for—"

But the boy's wine-stained lips were already on mine, acidic tongue prying and probing into my mouth. Before I could push him away, a voice boomed behind me.

"What in God's name is going on here?"

I turned back to find Pastor Wendell looming in the doorway, eyes dark with judgment. By the time I swiveled back to face Timothy, he had already scrambled away from me.

"It was her idea, Pastor!" He pointed a damning finger in my face. "She pulled me into her sinful ways!"

"I. . ." I was so confused by how quickly Timothy had turned on me that I couldn't find the words to deny it.

"It's okay, Timothy." Wendell stepped into the room. "Go down to the church and pray for God's forgiveness."

Timothy scurried away like a rat fleeing a flood as Pastor Wendell circled me on the floor. "I see the evil resides in *you* today, Abigail."

I shook my head. "I'm not evil."

"No. You're not." Wendell crouched in front of my face, lifting the wine bottle and squinting at it. "Did you know that when wine has not yet been blessed by me, it is purely poison?"

My hands clutched my stomach, suddenly worried about the gurgling within.

"That's what your sister Candace is. Poison, infecting everyone she comes into contact with. Then that person infects the next person, and the next one, until the whole flock is sick with corruption. Until God abandons us all." Wendell stood from his crouch and offered me his hand. "Do you wish to be saved, Abby?"

I nodded, taking his hand and getting to my feet.

"Then you must denounce your sister and keep your distance from her wicked ways. Do you understand?"

I loved my sister, but what if Pastor Wendell was right? What if the only way I could ever escape this place was to leave Candace behind? What if I could only save myself?

"Yes, Pastor," I replied in soft defeat.

"Good. Now, go downstairs and pray."

I sulked my way down the stairs to find Timothy whispering his prayers in the front pew. Surely what he said up in the rectory was a mistake, a misunderstanding. I needed him now more than ever. My meld-mate.

"Timothy. . ." I put a hand on his shoulder. "Can I pray with you?"

He shoved me away, venom in his voice. "Stay away from me. You're a snake in the garden, and I won't let you corrupt me."

Just as my heart had started to bloom, it was yanked out at the roots by the boy who loved me.

I look at him now, ten years older, and wonder if he still sees a snake in my scaly skin. But his eyes are bright as he asks: "Will you pray with me?"

He's betrayed me before, and I shouldn't trust him.

But maybe this is how our love story was always meant to happen. Maybe this is God's ultimate test.

Timothy smiles as I get down on my knees beside him. Pushing my palms together in the symbol of prayer feels like forcing two opposing magnets toward each other. It defies nature. I close my eyes and press my bloodstained palms together, ragged nails touching at the tips of my fingers.

God couldn't hear me down in the Bad Girl Box, but maybe he can up here.

I pray for something that's probably too much to ask for.

Something out of reach for a monster like me.

I pray for a happy ending.

The answer comes quickly, a cold *no* in the form of a chain suddenly slung around my throat. My eyes pop open and Timothy is behind me now, pulling the thurible chain tight. He's stronger than he looks, and his knee against my spine forces the tiny chain links to cut into my flesh.

"Depart, seducer!" Timothy cries.

My breath goes ragged. Maybe *this* is how it ends. Maybe I was always meant to be banished like the demon I am.

"Full of lies and cunning!"

Pastor Wendell looks down at me from the painting on the wall.

"Foe of virtue!"

His judging eyes remind me that I'm not here for happiness.

"Persecutor of the innocent!"

I'm here for punishment, and my good work is not yet done.

I reach backwards to scratch at Timothy's face. He screams, but doesn't relent.

"Give place, abominable creature!"

Darkness wraps around my vision like a friend.

"Give way, you monster!"

I push Death away. Not yet.

"Give way to Christ!"

My fingers find the crucifix hanging from Timothy's neck, and I yank Christ free. One blind jab sinks the long silver point into Timothy's flesh, and the chain around my neck goes slack.

I scramble away and turn back to see Timothy pawing at the crucifix jutting out of his neck, his eyes wild in dismay.

Crawling to my feet, I stumble to the altar and retrieve a golden chalice. Timothy is trying to speak, but his throat is gurgling red. I uncork the crucifix from his neck and press the chalice beneath the wound. Blood flows freely, desperate to escape this unworthy vessel as my golden goblet fills with thick red liquid.

"But with precious blood, as of a lamb. . ." I tilt the cup to my lips. It's even more bitter than the wine we shared together ten years ago. But I don't mind because this special juice fills me with fresh power, gives me life anew. "Unblemished and spotless."

Timothy falls backwards, bleeding out onto the rectory floor. I sip my drink as I watch him die, unmelded and alone. His final breath pairs nicely with my last gulp.

If that was a test, I think I passed.

I bring the heavy chalice over to the next door and use it like a hammer to smash the sturdy old knob, over and over again. Timothy's blood pulses through my veins, giving me newfound strength as the rusty metal comes loose and the old door swings open.

I can taste the cold air outside, stone steps leading up toward the heavens.

My final ascension begins.

CHAPTER NINETEEN

Austin waits for the sound of footsteps to fade up and away before he cracks the armoire door open. Stepping out first, his sneaker slips in a pool of blood before he regains his balance. Once Fiona and Mateo are out behind him, they all stare at Timothy's still-warm corpse on the floor.

The youth pastor's bone-pale skin matches the whites of his wide eyes.

Austin can't help thinking and saying: "We could've stopped it." It was hard to tell who was killing who from inside the armoire, hearing all the gasping and gurgling, but Candy Cain clearly won in the end.

"We only would've gotten in her way," Fiona says. "You know that."

He tries to shake off the guilt as he looks to the door Candy Cain just broke through. A set of stone steps leads up toward the belfry. It reminds him of the storm-door steps in the cellar where she lived for all those years.

Candy Cain is free now.

Fiona is still focused on the dead youth pastor. "At least his plan worked."

She's right. They're free now too. Austin exhales with relief. "Let's get the hell out of here."

"Amen. Again." Fiona starts toward the door leading back to the classroom, and Austin's right behind her when he hears Mateo over his shoulder.

"Wait."

He turns back to see Mateo staring at his own reflection in the mirror above the small altar, clearly having some kind of emo moment.

"You okay?" Austin asks.

Mateo's eye never leaves the mirror as he says the last thing Austin's expecting to hear him say: "I think we should follow her."

It's so absurd that a little laugh actually escapes Austin's mouth. "You're kidding, right?" But Mateo isn't kidding, so Austin asks: "Why?"

Mateo finally turns to face him. "I don't want to see this reminder in the mirror every day and wonder if she's gonna come back to finish the job."

Mateo's bandaged eye shows the physical trauma while his good eye carries the emotional kind. Austin knows he's asked a lot of his brand-new boyfriend today, but what Mateo's asking for now is damn near suicide.

Which is why Fiona is furiously shaking her head. "This is a very bad idea, guys. We have an out, we should take it."

Austin knows she's right. Fiona's always right. But instead of taking the out, he takes Mateo's hand. "You trusted me by coming here. It's my turn to trust you. If this is what you need, then I'm with you. We'll end it, together."

Mateo wraps his arms around Austin and squeezes so hard it hurts, but Austin doesn't care. Especially when he hears those three words spoken into his ear. "I love you."

Austin's never felt more sure of anything in his life as he speaks them right back. "I love you too."

A deep sigh from Fiona interrupts the moment. "Okay, fine, you sweet dumb idiots. Let's go follow the killer upstairs to certain doom, I guess." She passes her cane along with the silver staff to Mateo before turning to Austin. "But you're gonna have to carry my ass because I'm done with goddamn stairs today."

"Okay." Austin steels himself. "Let's kill Candy Cain."

Mateo leads the way up the steps, silver staff pointed out in a defensive stance, while Austin follows with Fiona on his back. It's a tight spiral upward into the church spire, where the only way out is down.

CHAPTER TWENTY

The sky is dusky red as Pastor Wendell emerges into the open-air belfry. He circles around the big bell toward the low exterior wall, holding the cell phone out. It's more like a hand-held computer, really, but he manages to plug *9-1-1* into the device and hit *Send*.

The phone is ringing, thank God. He loves his church, but he's not destined to die here. He will be saved by a voice on high.

"9-1-1, what is your emergency?"

"Yes, I need help." He skips right to the most important part. "I'm at the Nodland Church of Righteous Abso—"

Beep-beep in his ear as the line cuts out.

Wendell frantically presses his fingers against the keyboard, but the screen is black and lifeless, battery dead.

"Fuuuck!" he screams into the cold air, throwing the useless device off the roof.

What options does he have now?

He can't go back down those steps to face the children he just abandoned. They summoned that monster back from Hell. It's their cross to bear, not his.

But there's no other way off this spire, unless. . .

His eyes land on the bronze bell at the center of the belfry. There's a long rope attached to it, hanging all the way down into the church below so that Timothy can ring it by hand every Sunday.

Poor Timothy, who's probably dead by now.

But it's not Wendell's fault! He's been a good mentor to the boy, and surely that pure young soul is headed toward Heaven.

Wendell reaches for the rope, careful not to slip and fall into the pit below. When he finally gets it in his grasp, he tests to make sure it can withstand his weight. More grateful than ever for his sleight frame, he sways off his feet, dangling in the air.

He begins his descent slowly, ever so slowly, with one hand over the other. Keeping his legs wrapped loosely around the rope, his arms are already getting tired. The downside of that sleight frame is a distinctive lack of arm strength.

Still, he's doing it. He's going to get out of here. All he has to do is stay focused on—

A tug on the rope above makes his hand slip off. He nearly falls, but latches back on and releases the breath that lodged in his throat.

More tugging as someone is pulling the rope back up.

He cranes his neck up to see the shadowy figure with stringy hair as her voice echoes down the belfry.

"O little town of Bethlehem, how still we see thee lie!"

No, no, no.

Wendell scrambles, hand over hand, trying to climb down faster than he's being pulled up, but she's pulling so hard, so fast.

"Above thy deep and dreamless sleep, the silent stars go by!"

He's trying to move faster than his body can keep up, and another slip makes the rope burn against his palm, drawing blood. Wendell cries out, hugging his arms around the rope and giving up on his descent. He just holds tight for dear life while Candy Cain heaves the rope like a demented sailor, singing her shanty.

"Yet in thy dark streets shineth the everlasting light!"

How can she be so strong? He knows the answer, doesn't he? It's demonic strength, and with her sister dead, all that evil must be concentrated in one vessel.

But hadn't he decided they were the two witnesses from Revelation, sent by God to signal the end times?

He can't even keep track of his own mythologies. All he knows is that Candy Cain is pulling him across the belfry's edge now, lifting him by his collar and plopping him on his feet to face her. That mangled mug looks like someone took a blowtorch to a Picasso.

"The hopes and fears of all the years. . ."

Candy Cain wraps the end of the rope around his neck, over and over. Her breath is putrid with decay as she sings in his face.

". . . are met in thee tonight."

Pastor Wendell looks into her bloodshot eyes,

searching for the demonic presence or apocalyptic prophet that possesses this half-dead human. This may be the only chance he gets, and he can't leave this earthly realm without an answer to the question that has plagued him for so many years. . .

CHAPTER TWENTY-ONE

"What in God's name are you?" Pastor Wendell asks.

With the monster in my grasp, I'm finally ready to use my own words.

No more Christmas carols or Bible verses.

The last thing he hears will be my voice as I stare into his corrupt soul and speak.

"I am Abby. I am Candace. I am every child you made feel naughty. And when I kill you, God will sing."

The little man trembles, and my bare toes feel suddenly wet. I look down to see the puddle of pee spreading out over the stone floor from beneath the pastor's robe.

I put the fear of God into him.

A gift returned.

Now comes the reckoning.

I wrap my arms around Pastor Wendell, squeezing tight. He must think it's a hug because he mutters a weak, "I forgive you."

"I didn't ask," I whisper back.

He still doesn't realize that I'm here to end us both as

I step toward the big bell, ready to tip our tangled bodies over the belfry's edge. I don't know what I am, but I'm ready meet whatever maker might be waiting on the other side.

"Don't jump!" A plea from the doorway.

The voice makes me pause because I know it. I know *her*.

The girl who sat with me in front of the Christmas tree and said, "You don't have to do this." The girl who said, "We can get you help."

I didn't believe her then, but something in me wants to now as I turn to face the girl with the cane.

CHAPTER TWENTY-TWO

The words leapt from Fiona's lips before she could think, and now Austin and Mateo are looking at her with "Why?!" etched in their faces.

This whole nightmare was about to resolve itself before their eyes with Candy Cain taking Pastor Wendell down with her, but Fiona couldn't let that happen. That wouldn't be justice.

The fact that Candy Cain actually paused at Fiona's plea means there just might be some hope left after all for the girl in red and white striped pajamas.

"It doesn't have to end this way," Fiona says. "We know what he did, but he doesn't deserve to die."

Pastor Wendell breathes a sigh of relief. "Thank you, child."

"You're not my father, dickhead." Fiona glares at the pastor. "He was shot in the heart by your badge-toting henchman." She stomachs that rage before refocusing her attention on Candy Cain. "That's why Pastor Wendell deserves to rot in prison for the rest of his unholy life."

Wendell's face goes pale, Candy Cain still gripping him tightly at the edge of a very long fall. Fiona slowly glides to Candy Cain's side, careful not to spook her. It feels like approaching a tiger in the wild as she tries to get the beast to meet her eyes.

"That was *your* punishment, wasn't it?" Fiona asks. "Trapped in that house for so many years?"

Those blood-red eyes snap to meet Fiona's. A small breakthrough.

"He should suffer too. Just like you. Just like his beloved Christ."

Candy Cain huffs angrily, lifting Wendell off his feet and dangling him over the edge.

Well, it was worth a shot.

"Lord, have mercy!" Wendell cries out.

Candy Cain's arms tremble, ready to release him. But she tosses the pastor safely to the belfry floor instead, letting him live.

Fiona can't believe it actually worked. Candy Cain chose not to kill. But she's coughing now and clutching her neck, which is oozing blood from Timothy's attack. Candy Cain waivers on her bare feet before collapsing on all fours.

Austin hurries over. "Let me help you."

"Thank you." Pastor Wendell reaches up a hand. But Austin just yanks the sash from around Wendell's neck and goes to Candy Cain instead.

"Austin," Mateo says. "Be careful."

Fiona watches as her brother gently wraps the sash around Candy Cain's neck wound to slow the bleeding. She bares her teeth like a feral dog being pet for the first time, but the poor girl is too drained, too beaten down to bite or fight this small act of compassion.

Pastor Wendell pulls himself up by the low exterior wall, resting there as he paws at the rope still tangled around his neck. "If someone can help me untangle this, I vow to humbly accept my penance. Send me to prison that I might find more souls in need of saving."

Fiona squints at this. "You never know when to shut up, do you, Pastor?"

She grabs the silver staff from Mateo and flips it sideways to bar Wendell's path.

"Fiona," Austin says. "What are you doing?"

"He's just gonna find a new flock, Austin." Fiona's surprised by the dark thoughts flowing through her mind, the things she's prepared to do. It makes her feel crazy, until Mateo steps beside her, putting his hands on the staff next to hers.

"It's true," he says. "This pious parasite caused way more damage than Candy Cain ever could."

Wendell gasps at the accusation, rising to his feet in front of the low wall. "How dare you compare me to that monster!"

Austin looks at the weak girl slumped on the ground in front of him. Not a monster. Just a child. He takes his place beside his sister, all three of them gripping the silver staff, pressing it against Wendell's chest like the bar on a rollercoaster he can't get off.

The pastor challenges the heathen teens with more scripture. "Blessed are those who are persecuted for righteousness' sake. . ." Wendell grits his teeth. ". . . for theirs is the kingdom of Heaven."

Their hands tighten on the silver staff, three souls melding in one divine purpose.

Austin squints into the holy man's eyes. "You really believe you're the Second Coming, don't you?"

Wendell nods, filled with God-like confidence. "I know I am."

Fiona shrugs. "Well, good luck getting a third."

Six arms thrust forward in unison, ramming the staff against Pastor Wendell's chest, and he topples over the low wall with the rope still tight around his neck.

The trio cranes their heads over the edge to watch him scream all the way down. When the rope goes taught ten feet from the ground, the force is so great that Wendell's head is yanked from his body like a Christmas popper as the bell rings bright. His headless corpse crashes through the manger roof, slamming down on baby Jesus in his crib as a shower of blood splashes up against the nativity guests.

"Happy Birthday," Mateo says.

The first thing Fiona feels in the aftermath is righteous absolution.

The second thing she feels is hot breath right over her shoulder.

All three of them turn to face Candy Cain, back on her feet with hellfire in her eyes.

CHAPTER TWENTY-THREE

They ruined my death.

I was ready to end this wretched life, but now I'm standing in front of these three children who killed for me.

These three children who avenged me and my sister.

These three kings who gave me the greatest gift I could ever ask for.

I stretch my arms out toward them, and this time it *is* for a hug, but I stumble on my feet. The one they call Fiona catches me.

"It's okay, I've got you," she says. "Why don't we sit down and rest for a minute?"

Rest sounds nice.

Fiona guides me to the low wall. I swing my legs over the edge, and she gasps, but I'm not going to jump. I just like the view. They all join me, sitting side by side with our feet dangling high above Main Street.

The tolling of the bell has brought the children of Nodland out from the shadows. They must have been hiding, waiting until *ding-dong*, the Wendell is dead.

The young ones climb up onto the firetruck, laughing

and playing. Making snow angels and snowmen. Being kids.

The waitress bursts out of the diner below. "Oh my God!" Her eyes move from the headless pastor up the bloody rope to the belfry. "Are you all okay?!"

"Be down in a minute, Grace!" Austin calls down to her. "Can you pour us three more hot chocolates?"

Mateo gives him a nudge, motioning toward me.

"Right. Better make that four!"

Grace just nods in shock as she heads back into the diner.

Hot chocolate.

My tongue can't recall the taste, but I remember that I like it.

For ten long years, I've been trapped in a cold nightmare that's finally over. As the sun sets over Nodland and Christmas Day comes to an end, a lurking fear grips my heart. At least I've finally found my voice to ask: "What comes next?"

"December 26th," Fiona replies. "You're gonna love it. But more importantly. . ." She places her hand on mine and asks, "What do you want us to call you now?"

I feel a pinching at my armpits as I'm suddenly aware that my red and white striped pajamas are too tight. They don't fit me anymore because I'm not Abby or Candace or the Candy Cain Killer, and I'll never be a child of Nodland again.

When I look at Fiona and Austin and Mateo beside me, I feel that fire inside again. Only it's different now, burning not in my gut, but closer to my heart. The flames of wrath and vengeance have given way to something softer, warmer.

I know I'm asking too much, that Santa himself could never grant a wish so great.

Not to me.

But I ask anyway.

"Can you call me 'sister?'"

I'm ready for rejection, destined to be forsaken.

But Fiona is sweeter than Santa as she smiles brightly. "Okay, sister. Ready to go home?"

That H-word used to mean Hell to me, but maybe it can be different now.

Maybe it can mean "hope."

I open my mouth to speak, but the lump in my throat chokes me up as the word stumbles out.

"Ho-ho-home."

A tear rolls down my cheek, the first I've shed in so many years.

I can't wipe it away, don't want to lose this feeling.

I let it freeze.

STOP ■

ACKNOWLEDGMENTS

This is all your fault. Seriously. Sequels don't happen without support for the first book. That's why my first debt of gratitude is to you, dear reader, forever and always. Thank you so much for loving Candy Cain as much as I do and giving me this opportunity to deepen her story.

To all the reviewers, Bookstagrammers, podcasters, booksellers, librarians, and every other manner of book-folk who dedicate their time and energy to helping readers find the right book.

You're amazing, every single one of you. Extra enormous thanks to Sadie Hartmann and Ashley Saywers for including the first book in their December 2023 Nightworms box. Special shoutout to Stephanie Gagnon of Books in the Freezer Podcast for suggesting that sequel books should have a "Previously On" section. I hope my cheeky rhymes did the trick.

I wrote this book during a challenging transitional period of my life. Gratefully, my new community in Mesa, AZ is filled with some incredible people who quickly made me feel at home. Especially my dear friend in joyful healing, Heidi Selover. The Devil and God might be raging inside us, but at least they can hold a harmony.

I remain in awe of the utterly incomparable Alan Lastufka, who infuses so much passion into every printed word that Shortwave puts out. Marc Vuletich once again took my twisted vision for cover art and knocked it straight into the heavens. See you in Hell, bud. Speaking of, thanks to Nancy LeFever and Erin Foster for making sure I kept my Hells capped and Bibles versed. To my agent, Dan Milaschewski, thank you for always taking the long view on my career.

Mom and Dad, thanks for sending me to Catholic school. I obviously learned a lot. But the heart of this story has always been the loving bond between siblings, and I couldn't have written it if I didn't have the best in the world. Love you, Steve and Kim.

Writing a sequel is a scary prospect. You don't want to taint the original, but you do want to ramp up the mayhem and find new surprises along the way. I hope you'll agree that this new beginning is the ending Candy Cain deserves. Then again, it's not really up to me. Lord knows she's the queen.

Slaymen,

Brian McAuley

ABOUT THE AUTHOR

Brian McAuley is a WGA screenwriter who has written everything from family sitcoms to horror films for major studios and networks. His debut novel *Curse of the Reaper* was named one of the Best Horror Books of 2022 by Esquire. In 2023, his holiday slasher novella *Candy Cain Kills* earned praise from Kirkus, Booklist, and Library Journal. His short fiction and nonfiction have appeared in Dark Matter, Nightmare, Shortwave, and Monstrous Magazines. Brian is a Clinical Assistant Professor of Screenwriting at ASU's Sidney Poitier New American Film School.

Connect with him on social media @BrianMcWriter

A NOTE FROM SHORTWAVE

Thank you for reading the fifth Killer VHS Series book! If you enjoyed *Candy Cain Kills Again*, please consider writing a review. Reviews help readers find more titles they may enjoy, and that helps us continue to publish titles like this.

For more Shortwave titles, visit us online...

OUR WEBSITE

shortwavepublishing.com

SOCIAL MEDIA

@ShortwaveBooks

EMAIL US

contact@shortwavepublishing.com

ALSO AVAILABLE FROM SHORTWAVE PUBLISHING

ALSO AVAILABLE FROM SHORTWAVE PUBLISHING

ALSO AVAILABLE FROM SHORTWAVE PUBLISHING

ALSO AVAILABLE FROM SHORTWAVE PUBLISHING

ALSO AVAILABLE
FROM
SHORTWAVE PUBLISHING

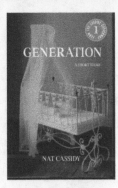